Local Hero

20 New Short Stories
from Cape Breton Island

"Peter enjoyed a good story. He enjoyed even more telling a good story and this after all was a dandy. It was a story that would outlive them all."

from "Local Hero"

Local Hero

20 New Short Stories
from Cape Breton Island

Edited by
Ronald Caplan

Breton Books

Local Hero © 2015 Breton Books

All rights to the individual stories belong to the authors. Our thanks for their permission to include them in this collection.

Photographs of Maureen Hull by David Hardy, Joyce Rankin by Blaine Aitkens, Dave Doucette and D.C. Troicuk courtesy Cape Breton University Press. Front Cover photograph by Ronald Caplan.

Editor: Ronald Caplan
Production Assistants: Bonnie Thompson and Sharon Hope Irwin
Layout: Fader Communications

We acknowledge the support of the Canada Council for the Arts for our publishing program. Canada Council for the Arts   Conseil des Arts du Canada

We recognize the support of the Province of Nova Scotia through Film and Creative Industries Nova Scotia. We are pleased to work in partnership with the Province of Nova Scotia to develop and promote our creative industries for the benefit of all Nova Scotians.    FILM & CREATIVE INDUSTRIES NOVA SCOTIA

We acknowledge the financial support of the Government of Canada through the Canada Book Fund for our publishing activities.   Canada

Library and Archives Canada Cataloguing in Publication

Local hero : 20 new short stories from Cape Breton Island / selected by Ronald Caplan.

ISBN 978-1-926908-36-6 (paperback)

    1. Short stories, Canadian (English)--Nova Scotia--Cape Breton Island.
2. Canadian fiction (English)--21st century. I. Caplan, Ronald, 1942-, editor
II. Title.

PS8329.5.C36L63 2015   C813'.010897169   C2015-904425-1

Printed in Canada

Contents

Carmel Mikol • And Then I Can See *1*
Carol Bruneau • Polio Beach *6*
Hector MacNeil • Local Hero *17*
Clive Doucet • The Gaelic Ship *23*
Maureen Hull • Finches *33*
D.C. Troicuk • Sin *40*
Dave Doucette • Carving Initials *49*
David Muise • Paste Wax *62*
Sue McKay Miller • Driving to Dolores *66*
Julie Curwin • Killing Agnes Donakowski *79*
Ellison Robertson • Anglers *89*
Tim Vassallo • Chainsaw *109*
Charlotte Musial • Old, Young Love *115*
Joyce Rankin • A Wagon Load *122*
Ruth Morris Schneider • Behind the Glass *127*
Larry Gibbons • To Catch a Coin *135*
Jigs Gardner • Owly Bob *143*
Teresa O'Brien • To Country Living *149*
Victor Sakalauskas • Wings of Tar *157*
Bill Conall • The Waiting Room *164*

The Writers *169*

Carmel Mikol

And Then I Can See

THE NIGHT THEY COME FOR HIM, he's barely getting air. Bent over the edge of the bed. That wool bedspread only comes out in the fall.

Out here we know everybody by the sound their car makes on the dirt road. I know he recognizes the Volunteer Fire Department truck coming up the hill along the east boundary of our land, a five-acre length of pine trees. He planted them twenty-five years ago; they stand twelve and fifteen feet now. Fifty of them, back when they were seedlings, fit in his hip sack. But he doesn't let on he knows they're coming.

"We're having trouble breathing, are we?" says the First Responder. He fumbles with the shirtsleeve and wraps a black cuff around my father's arm.

"I don't know how long. He doesn't tell us what he's feeling. It could have been days." My mother dialed 911 half an hour ago. He didn't want her to. They argued, but she did finally.

The proper ambulance comes from town a minute later. We hear it coming but wait for the paramedics to knock. Their uniforms are foreign; they move fast.

I follow behind the ambulance in my Jeep, the absurd red emergency lights smashing the trees and my windshield and the wide darkness of the rural road. We pass no other cars. It's quiet except for when they pull over to the side of the road and I pull over too waiting to find out why and assuming it means it's all over already and then I start crying in loud, ugly bursts that echo strangely in the car. No siren. Just the red lights.

We keep on after that though. Must have been hard getting

the IV in, all the frost heaves and turns. Had to pull over to hit the vein.

I'm not sure I remember it right.

I'm never good with this stuff. Always freeze in place when something happens.

That winter Bessie died, I hid in my room for days. I peeked from the curtains to watch my father lift her massive body with the tractor and bury her in a pit behind the barn where a backhoe chewed into the ground and left a black hole in the snow. She slipped on the ice and choked on the rope tethering her to the barn. Nobody was around to hear her struggle. It still makes me sick. It was a real blow to buy a new milking cow in the middle of the winter, my father said.

Once my cat got caught in a blizzard. We put her in a crate by the woodstove and I sat there staring at her. I wouldn't pet her in case she was already dead. In the end, she made it and I felt bad I didn't help her more.

There are people who have it and people who don't. My big sister kind of loves all that. She used to pick up snakes and examine dead frogs, poke at her cuts and pick at her scabs, get her hands into everything. She should have been the one to move home when our father got sick. But it was me.

I was in traffic when I answered the phone. He said, "Pull over." There was a blue Suburban in front of me. I almost nicked it when I yanked the wheel to the shoulder.

"It's cancer. They said three weeks. We need you to come home."

You come around the cove, up that big hill where the moon spills out over St. Ann's Bay and shatters up against the gypsum cliffs. You lose cell service right there. Then around Goose Cove and it all quiets down. Dirt road on the left. Take it for a few miles and you're home. You don't ever forget the way even if it's been years.

I arrive at midnight and the house is dark. My mother wakes up when she hears the door.

"You're here. You're here. You're here." Her arms hold me. As if she wasn't sure I'd come. As if she doesn't know me.

"Where's Dad?"

"Get some rest. You must be exhausted."

I don't sleep well in my kid bed. It's too quiet after the city. Real dark like the basement where the laundry machines are in my apartment off Bloor. Across the hall the bed creaks every time he turns. I know he isn't sleeping either.

In the morning I make pancakes from a box with Aunt Jemima syrup and burn the butter a little. The way he asks me to.

"Your mother will need help," he says from across the table. He cuts the pancakes into squares and eats one. "The spare tractor keys are up there in that mug. You'll need to know that."

My mother's gone for errands in town. I stare at the plate in front of me but never touch it.

"I'll make sure to straighten up the shop before." He eats another square then goes to throw up.

Afterwards he scrapes the remains of his plate into a dish and leaves it by the screen door. The neighbour's dog comes for it if the squirrels don't get it first. I do the dishes. It's a morning routine we will repeat for weeks.

They say it's pneumonia and he has to stay. After a night in Emergency they move him to Palliative. I become obsessed with predicting the day he will die.

"Any day now," the doctor says. Another week passes. And another.

"One stubborn heart."

After these check-ups, my father nods and goes back to the TV where nothing plays. The grey screen reflects his bed, the armchair next to him where my mother is stationed, and the bench where I sit cross-legged working on something in my notebook. He's generally quiet the whole time. People who come to visit call him brave. But I mostly remember a sort of resolution. Like he'd made a deal: if he goes quietly then something else will happen in return, but I'm not sure what.

Later when I write his obituary I won't say he "battled with cancer" or "lost his fight" with it. I simply write he "died from cancer" and that's it. Why he hung on so much longer than they all predicted is never explained. But I guess he had his reasons. People always do.

In the Unit Library I find a book listing five signs of imminent death: blue fingernails, yellowing skin, hallucinations, laboured breathing, the fifth one I forget. I check his fingernails that night. They are pink and clean. I've never seen his hands so clean. They were always tanned and cracked and hemmed in dark lines of dirt. But he hasn't worked for months.

He does get strange near the end. Starts talking about his mother. Asks me what her middle name was. He stares at the peach-coloured wall in front of his bed for a long time trying to remember it. But I don't know either. They kept her dishes on the top shelf so no one else would touch them. She washed them with different soap and no one ever hugged her. Tuberculosis took her when he was eleven.

Once he says, "Ask her to come here." But of course she isn't there.

Later, my meditation coach will tell me my weak lungs are my connection to the grandmother I've never known and I will believe her and like the idea of it, but wonder if I carry my father's leukemia somewhere in my bones too.

The day he dies my mother and I are eating strawberries in the Palliative Unit cafeteria. Talking to a man whose mother is a few doors down the hall from us. Slurping the strawberries out of the milk and laughing about something I read in the newspaper. Drinking the last bit of milk turned pink from the berries and letting our spoons land with a clink in the empty bowls. Sauntering down the hallway with bellies full, smiling at the nurses we know by name. And when we get back to the room, he is gone.

"What are you waiting for?"
"I can't see."
"Yes you can."

"It's too dark."

"Your eyes will adjust. Just wait." My father stops walking.

"I'm scared." I must be four or five years old.

"Nothing to be scared of. Snow's too deep this time of year," he says.

All afternoon I was building mini villages with blocks of wood that fell from his workbench, plowing sawdust roads in the floors, huddling up near the woodstove with a barn cat and watching him work at the lathe, curls of maple flying out from his chisel and snowing down on my make-believe world. When we go out to walk home for supper, it's black dark. No moon. I didn't expect it; you know the way time passes when you're a kid.

I'm standing out there, both little feet in just one of my father's boot prints. All the nothingness and the loud sound of the unknown. My father keeps saying: wait and see.

Slowly the snow turns kind of grey and up at the top of the hill that tall pine that marks the northern edge of our property emerges navy blue against the sky (which is why we still call her Mama Pine) and my father's jacket is almost red, but only because I know it's red, and the tiniest glimmers of gold come through the trees from the house and I smell the smoke from the wood stove in the kitchen which makes me see it kind of purple in the cold air, and my breath and my father's breath show up like that too. And then I can see.

I step forward till I reach him and attach my hand to the bottom hem of his jacket. We walk together up the long hill to the house.

Carol Bruneau

Polio Beach

WE'RE OLDER NOW, MY COUSINS AND I—the cousins who would occupy my mind. A couple of us have children grown up and far-flung, who themselves have little reason to come here. My own reasons for coming dwindle steadily; by the end of this day they'll have dwindled to none. But this bears no thinking of, just now. Taking a beach break—a respite in the sad business of burying an old aunt, the last of our mothers' family, and divvying up the "spoils," her worldly goods—we walk in solitude, my husband and I. On this windy crescent locked between cliffs, the furthest merging with the town of my mother's birth and its slag heap's glacial outline, we walk to put in time this dark July afternoon.

It could easily be mistaken for early spring, the sea a roiling dark blue: whitecaps, breakers, bits of plastic bobbing on them. Spray stings the air—with a foulness, we realize, as the dog noses the tidemark and a tilting sign anchored in concrete comes in view: Warning. Outfall. A sludgy current froths, waves flinging murk onto the sand—ribbons of toilet paper, not kelp—this once-pristine beach where we swam as kids and my mother and her sisters before us. Abandoned, it's a floating landfill. The dog roots at the pink plastic of what could be a prosthesis—a doll's leg—then darts around a diaper, the detritus of people too busy stumbling through the days to cover any tracks.

It's as if the sun-splashed shore in my memory never existed: scalding sand under untroubled feet and blankets weighted with stones, oranges, towels, shivering bodies. The only evidence of what was is a charred stretch of boardwalk passing a boggy oasis of alders, burnt wood littering the battered dune. Vandalism or some party's bonfire gone wild? This can't be the place we swam, can it? I call to my husband—but he's out of hearing, hastily leashing the dog, sidestepping something no doubt gross. It can't be the place. Yet it is, its ruin a large, fairly final nail in the lid of a chest of memories soon to be set adrift. Having come from Halifax, I'm missing home.

To everything there is a season. Still, feeling relief that, having quit coming here years ago, Aunt Flo was spared seeing her old shore "go to pot," I linger, longing to find something unchanged—evidence of finer days. And there it is: the brackish pond behind the fouled dunes, its stream emptying into the sea, the suck of its current so strong it still cuts the beach in two. Unbreachable now as then, it offers proof that the filthiest spot is indeed where we spent hot afternoons—hours of *hen-rooster-chicken-duck*—rewarded afterwards with Orange Crush from the crossroads store, its dripping cooler. Wasn't life sweet, in the days when Ma cut oranges into dories—*Rory's in the dory, and he can't get out*—and sprinkled on the white death?

Turning my back on it, I take a last look at the nearest cliff, blunt sandstone that once glinted like a Fat Archie rolled in sugar—in my mind's eye, at least—and pick my way over the spray-pocked sand. Such are childhood's mirages, and the feelings that come, at a certain age, of having occupied some lost universe.

Black clouds meet the horizon. Spray beads the car's windshield and my husband flicks on the wipers; the engine throws off heat. The dog yawns, curling up on the back seat. "It wasn't always so disgusting," I say, a feckless protest, and again the past seeps forward in dribs and drabs—as if it's dammed and pouring out too fast would exhaust it, a reservoir emptying like the pond back there, where stories lie of this or that one drowning, learning to skate or swim, of the model boats my grandfather built and tested before anyone had cars. Isn't the past shaped of exactly these things?

"We used to say you'd catch polio from that stream," I tell my husband, smiling at how it brings what's lost to life. "It was so frigging cold, we believed it too—you believe anything when you're six, I guess."

Flo's little bungalow is as she left it: the living room with its floral upholstery, plants dropping leaves. How did we forget to water them, certain she'd return from hospital? "A bird that tough makes you think they'll last forever," says Gregory, her only nephew.

On the table lie the reception's leftovers: store-bought finger foods, an extravagant Tim's cake which no one's had the nerve to cut—foods Flo herself would avoid, disliking chocolate and the prospect of sharing germs with a roomful of people. A staunch wielder of fork and knife, Flo. My cousin from away, Felicity, uncorks a bubbly white which Flo would've snubbed for a red. "Thought I'd go all out," says Gregory, self-congratulatory, helping himself to a large slab of the cake, his doing. The last of our kin in the town, he'll miss Flo the most. So good of *you* to have stayed for her, the rest of us say—Felicity, Grete, also come from out of province, and I. Silently my husband drains his glass and leashes the dog for a walk, though rain begins to streak the windows.

Such good care you took of her, we agree—though it wasn't Gregory the hospital called with Flo's diagnosis or her passing, wondering about arrangements. His phone oddly, mysteriously, out of range.

"You've had so much to deal with, Greg," repeats Grete who, like Felicity, has always nursed an attachment to down-homers, the town itself no place you'd visit without good reason, unlike the misty sea- and mountain-hugged villages north and west of here. Yet we came, as often and as faithfully as we could, staying close to Flo in ways we didn't, haven't, with each other.

"To Flo." Felicity raises her glass—one of our aunt's, a miniscule, crystal sherry glass in which even the chips are ladylike. Grete laughs, dangling hers, already emptied.

"God yes, to Flo!" booms Gregory, and Felicity busies herself topping everyone up. Her green, almond-shaped eyes already register the dust overtaking knick-knacks and pictures with names masking-taped to their undersides. Trinkets and tokens of a life of comings and goings in rising then weakening waves like radio signals, or rings on the pond's surface.

"Well, it's too bad she missed the summer."

"Loved a beach day, didn't she though."

"Damn right—never gave a crap how cold it was, either."

"Just peel off, jump in and give'r."

Maybe it's the wine, though I'm wondering where my husband's got to, keen to leave us to our grieving. Because I'm laughing and nodding, though the Flo I knew was not such a swimmer but a cautious breaststroker who hugged the shore, permed curls snug inside her bathing cap.

"She saved my life, you know," our cousin brags and Felicity and Grete snort—"Here we go"—recalling when we were kids and he locked himself in a fridge. But he shakes his head, and I feel the echo of icy currents, the kind pale as stretchmarks over the sea's calm. So the past comes back.

The scorching sun marooned his ma and mine and Flo on their blankets, while he and I plovered and hopscotched—the ocean too frigid for more than toe-dipping, cold enough to give a kid like me polio, teased Gregory, who knew how to swim. Since I didn't, I was happy snuggling close to Ma, sucking on a Rory-dory while Aunt Glenna tugged up her suit and rolled over to bake. Throwing fistfuls of sand then dipping his blue plastic pail, Gregory threatened to fling it—*Polio, polio, who wants polio! A polio bomb!* A joke? Ma gritted her teeth. Auntie Flo, who didn't have children, ducked under her towel.

Glenna's laugh switched to a shriek at Gregory's selective dousing. Why wasn't Ma jumping up to give her first aid? Take her temperature, hold her hand, give mouth-to-mouth resuscitation? The things a nurse did in a bad situation. Ma's smile was knotted; she rolled her eyes at Flo. I guessed what this could be about: Ma said polio was in the hospital, not the ocean. She should know, she had a friend who limped from catching it as a child. Vaccination was a word I knew from school. A drop of something pink on a sugar cube? A round scab on someone's upper arm, like a brand from a car's lighter, I speculated, having watched *Bonanza* and my aunts lighting cigarettes off one. What I also knew was that kids got sick, the children's hospital full of them in oversized cribs and iron lungs, kids in casts and in wheelchairs, on crutches and in leg braces. Ma said so.

"It's no joke," she said, her voice enough to put us in a cast—well, Gregory, who it was aimed at. "You never joke about disease." She glared so hard that silent Glenna scowled and drop-jawed Gregory. Gregory who could do no wrong, grabbed his pail to refill it. "Don't," his ma said, and after a while the sisters leaned back watching the slow, glassy swells wash ashore, gulls bob, and a tiny white fishing boat haul nets—the sea a perfect blue thunder that rolled us with it. My small feet shaped waves in the sand, the light through my eyelids the red of a plastic bucket drying in the sun under that fixed, cloudless sky.

"Your mother could be a hardass, eh," Gregory says—a joke except for the way his eyes cross mine, this middle-aged, balding man who does caretaking for a living. "Some serious, wasn't she."

But that afternoon I remember her laughing, pointing down the beach to the stream glinting in the sun. "If you were going to catch anything," she said, "it'd be from there." Both her sisters, peeling back the flaps of their bathing caps after one last, futile attempt at a dip, nodded, Glenna adding that just that March a kid had almost died going through the pond's ice. For some sort of emphasis she slapped her quivering thighs, Ma shaking her head and Flo mimicking their complaints about orange-peel dimples, till Gregory, stabbing the sand with his plastic shovel, complained of thirst. Refusing Flo's thermos of juice, he yelled for pop, then whined to go home. I zipped my lips, of course. It was Greg's way or the highway, Ma once said, nothing at Aunt Glenna's run the way Ma ran things at home, like in a hospital—everything having its time and place—except in the case of the ashtray beside my uncle's chair and the bird that drank from a glass atop their TV, bobbing and dipping "till the cows come home," Glenna said.

"I could stay forever," my aunt moaned, a sand flea hopping from her girded stomach to Flo's knee.

"I-want-pop! Give-me-pop!" Gregory ranted louder and louder. "I'm dying here, I'm dyin'!" His feet squeaked, kicking sand. His fists pounded the blanket. Nestling closer to Ma, I clung to her neck. "Orange Crush, Oraaange Crussshhhh," Glenna mimicked the sea. "Give us five more minutes, Greg—you can do that, right? Just a little longer." Sighing, "Run off now. Just for a bit. See what you can find."

"You too, Marcie," Mother nudged me. "Keep him company—just for a sec." I knew that voice: it was for yet more catching up, never enough time to hear all about who'd died, gotten sick or suffered other awful things since the sisters had last been together. Its impatience made me miss my dad in Halifax; he'd have taken my hand and run along too.

"See what treasures you find," coaxed Flo, the one who'd never married. "I'll bet there's treasures—jewels," Ma said over Glenna's whisper, something-something about their other sister, the one they were missing, stuck in Ontario.

"Try thataway, maybe?" Ma waved us towards the spot good for finding beach glass, best of all the blue of VapoRub jars. "And pick some shore coal!" she called cheerfully. The three of them already moving closer, Glenna sifting sand through her fingers: the sign of rapt attention.

"I don't agree with pop," I heard Ma say, squelching my sugary hopes. Gregory was out of earshot, tearing towards the stream. Its banks a proven trove of feathers and seashells and, once, a dried squid as papery as onionskin, the bead of one eye staring up.

Veering that way, dropping our buckets, we toed the hem of sea foam, felt the undertow grate our heels. "The frigger's a time machine!" Gregory yelped as the beach and the froth roared us backwards. Pebbles glittered. Gulls wheeled. My feet felt webbed and numb, my heart thumping as the waves dragged then shoved us back to dry sand. "C'mon, Bacteria," he called me, making a beeline now for the stream that swung and chiseled its way to the surf. Its banks caved under the giant steps he took, trouncing them. "Josh-wah fought the battle of Jericho, Jericho, Jericho," he yelled tunelessly, stomping the dark sand as fast as the current could sweep it away. "And the walls come a-tumbling down!" I sang out, hanging back. Its gold glint deepening to the brown of cola, rank with eelgrass and mussel mud it smelled brinier than the sea. "Is it poison?" I hollered, my question lost to his splashing.

Gingerly I parked my bum on its sandy ledge, a cool, wet bench. Light enough to sit without toppling it, I kicked my feet, watched the tickling yellowness glide over them. Whooping, Gregory scooped up armfuls of it, geysers flashing down over me. "Gonna be a cripple! Marcie the cripple! Won't be able to walk 'cause the polio'll take your legs off!"

It felt the same as when a wave had once knocked me under: the wanting to cry but being too scared to, the sting up my nose. Down the beach—far enough that her bathing cap looked white instead of pink, like the head of one of Flo's hatpins, not the dahlia it mimicked—Ma waved. Standing, Aunt Flo draped something over herself; shielding her eyes, she waved too. Gregory's ma was still pressed to the sand, so it really looked as if there were just Ma and Flo, Glenna no more than a beach bag or deflated water wings. My cousin went on splashing and jeering, though his teasing eased into something gentler, brotherly—didn't they all say he was as good as a brother?

"Frig off—you won't get the polio. Don't cry." His sunburnt face darkened under the cruising shadow of a gull. "But you don't wanna know what's in the pond, Bacteria." Sucking in his lips, he made a somber, popping sound. A guy had drowned in there when our mothers were small, he said, and a kid too, late last winter, trying to skate. They were never found, he said, with the gravity of grownups unaware we were listening.

Gregory had a habit of talking through his hat, Ma said.

With a wild yelp, he raced off when the sand under him let

go—the ground in a cartoon earthquake—causing me to fall in. The yellow only came up to my frill, but next was quicksand—the stuff that buried people alive—the stream tickling my ribs as my cousin waded near its mouth. Filling his pail repeatedly, he flung the water back at itself, then dropped to his knees, digging feverishly in the sand. No matter how fast he scooped it out, the hole filled in. From a distance our mothers' laughter filtered down to us. Ma had stretched out again, she and Glenna lying flat as kippers in a tin. Wrapped in her towel, Flo was sitting up.

Gregory waded out deeper and deeper, to where the yellowness thinned, buckling over itself in thick, fast wrinkles. I could tell by that far-off laughter that Ma and my aunts were having fun, even as I sank deeper. But it was okay: I still had legs and feet, the yellowness no different from peeing underwater, a warming, cosy clamminess. Polio lived in hospitals, not brooks. I slapped the surface with both hands as a wave pushed closer. Its tingling cold swelled around me, a tingly delight as it retreated.

But where was Gregory? Where had he got to? His pail twirled on the ripples, bouncing on the froth. As if buckets grow on trees, Ma would say—and pop and chocolate bars too. Once, well out of Glenna's hearing, she'd called him spoiled. The thought of salty sweetness filled me, until a wave knocked me backwards, pushing bubbles up my nose, and through its gurgling thunder I heard myself howl.

But I was all right, and crawled onto hot sand.

Out in the swells a bird was fishing—diving, sinking, beating the water with its wings—something I'd seen more times than Ma and them could shake a stick at, Gregory would say, meaning nothing special, nothing to turn your head. Eating sandwiches Flo packed, over and over we'd watched similar flashes and bobs of white, tiny fish wriggling from beaks.

Now what I saw was a paleness—the paleness of curls?—as I squirmed against the grit caught in my suit. Everyone said Gregory had such pretty hair, what a sin being wasted on a boy, even Ma said. Next there was a scream—a squawk—as pale and scratchy as the sand, a sound rolling in and rolling out. Too, too far away to be a person, to be him.

It was Flo who twigged to it, Flo who'd glanced over as he ventured out swinging his bucket. Who'd seen the waves tighten around him and, who knows, when his feet left bottom. It was Flo who broke from a trot into a dash; Glenna peeling herself from the blanket, hurtling forward, Ma too—all three having removed their bathing caps, despairing of a swim. They were fully-inflated water wings the way they skittered over the sand, wisps of it like smoke trailing them.

Somebody shrieked, the kind of shriek heard in scary movies, which I had yet to see. Perhaps it was Flo, petite but full-bosomed, the oldest of the sisters, waves zooming around her and breaking as she plunged in. The water past her chest, arms waving over her head as if flagging someone down. A wave smashed over top of her, and another.

No matter how I squinted, no matter how I stared, I could no longer see Gregory, that bird. But there was a shout, and there they were: Flo buoying a small flailing thing in her arms, sinking, bobbing, thrashing—Glenna frozen in the surf up to her neck. The noises she was making were like an animal's as Ma waded out, held onto her so the sea wouldn't take her too.

I'd seen the man earlier spreading out his towel below the dunes, taking off his shoes. Not noticing me he angled closer, flying past. Red bathing trunks. Dodging the stream, jack-knifing under the place where yellowness fanned into blue. Slicing through waves, his arms chopped the sea.

Glenna was screaming, screaming, screaming as he swam. The sea had moved the buoy that was Auntie Flo and my cousin farther and farther down the beach and out and out, so it wasn't hard to imagine them disappearing past the horizon like the fishing boat.

All I could do was close my eyes.

I remember the white string swinging from the man's trunks. I remember him carrying Gregory ashore, Flo staggering behind.

I remember the man pushing on Gregory's chest and my cousin barfing water. My aunt Glenna lying on the sand crying, then kissing them both—and Flo sitting on the beach, her head between her knees.

"He could've killed the two of them," Ma whispered later, out of their hearing.

I remember that Gregory got to drink all the Orange Crush and eat all the O'Henry bars and Scotties chips he wanted. He was the king of the castle that night, the two of us allowed to stay up past bedtime to watch *Bonanza*—it went without saying.

I remember Flo bending to kiss my forehead, trembling but patting my cheek as if nothing had happened.

"She said it herself, she'd thought we were goners. She told herself, 'Well, at least it'll be quick.'" Gregory rises stiffly, shakes out his legs, thick and white and a little pudgy in gym shorts. He disappears to the kitchen for a minute—we think it's to find more wine—but when he comes back he has a long brown envelope in his hands, legal-size. "No time like the present—guess we should get to it." He is the executor, of course.

I hear my husband come in, the scrabble of wet paws, the leash being hung, a hush.

Felicity's eyes water. Grete holds a cherry tomato between her long fingers; she takes forever bringing it to her mouth.

"Ah, Flo always did like you best, Greg," she laughs wryly, glancing around as if waiting for a bottle—a magic one—to appear. But there's just the empty one and a vase with her name on the bottom, already noted.

"She decided to leave everything…well, what can I say, you know it's all here, right? She signed it all over, what was I gonna do?"

The room goes silent. The well-kept house is a broken shell without Flo, we all know it, as is our shared past. From the kitchen there's just the sound of the dog licking herself and my husband trying to stay invisible.

"Yeah?" Grete's voice is harsher. Felicity looks stricken. Gregory natters now about power of attorney, responsibilities, doing his best. I am not surprised.

"She saved my life, for fuck sake," he says, and then something unexpected: "Here's the thing. The house? I'm signing it over—youse can all do with it what you like. I'm outta here, I hope. Been thinking of McMurray, Red Deer, Nanaimo, what the hell. This way you'll have somewhere to come to, how she would've wanted it, really. The least I can do."

The least and the most, finally, this unburdening of shored-up things lost, unsalvageable, their encumbrance no more ours than it ever was his: this is what he holds out.

Hector MacNeil

Local Hero

"How that devil of a bull never broke poor Sandy's back or never killed him I can not understand!"

Peter released the last words one at a time, letting them fall like blocks of firewood hitting the floor. Jim could feel his stomach knotting at the thought of what was coming. He'd heard it often enough in the last couple of weeks. Christ, he'd lived it. Peter looked over at Jim sitting by the window in the kitchen. "There is no doubt in my mind," he said again. "That boy sitting there saved his father's life."

Jim looked down at the floor, studied the sure black line between the blue and white tiles by his shoe. No one had been able to coax out of him more than a terse explanation of what had happened that day in the barnyard. Even old Peter had had to wait, gleaning details as they fell out accidentally like little pieces of glass from a splintered window.

Peter's account painted Jim as a kind of hero, but Peter wasn't there for the whole event. He'd only seen the end. Only Jim and his father Sandy knew the whole story, and today Jim's father had gotten out of the hospital.

His father had let out "the little bull" in order to clean out his stall just inside the door of the cow barn. The little bull was a runt, five years old and about half the size of a good-sized cow. He should have been gone long before but Sandy had a soft spot for that bull and treated it like a kind of pet. Jim always thought that it was because his dad had tried to castrate the bullock and botched it. He'd never admit to it but you could see it there as plain as day, one lone testicle hanging down where there should have been twins. Jim thought his father felt bad for the little bull, that's why he kept him. The damn thing would follow him around the barnyard like a big stupid dog. Jim was afraid of that bull although he tried hard not to let it show. His father should have gotten rid of him. Everyone thought so, most even said so. But that was Sandy. He had his ways, they'd say.

Jim was supposed to keep an eye on the bull for his father while he cleaned the stall. The damn bull would want to be nosing his way into the cow barn with Sandy stooped over shovelling out the manure. The bull was starting to act like a bull, starting to get, if not aggressive, then assertive, and even Sandy was getting a little bit careful of him. Jim was afraid of that bull. He'd gone into the tool shed to get an axe. He didn't know what he'd do with it, but if he was going to mind that bull, he knew he'd feel better if he had the axe in his hand.

He was in the tool shed when he'd heard the commotion in the cow barn, the bull bawling and his father shouting. The sound of his father's shovel hitting the wall of the barn and then a muffled thud of something soft hitting something solid, and then again and again. By the time Jim reached the cow barn, the little bull was staggering out over the threshold of the doorway with Jim's father hanging from his horn by his leather belt. The other horn was tangled in the heavy flannel jacket that his dad wore around the barn. Sandy's body had worked its way over the side of the bull's neck and hung there limp. Sandy's legs were askew, tangled in among the bull's front legs, tripping the bull as he stumbled out into the air. The little bull stood there trembling, froth and snot blowing from his nostrils and dripping down over Sandy's green barn jacket, and for the moment he seemed bewildered as to how to rid himself of this burden.

It wasn't until Jim was back in the tool shed that he felt the handle of the axe still clutched in his hand. He let the axe go clattering to the floor, grabbed the .22 off its rack and shoved the rifle up under his arm. He dumped the box of shells into his hand as he ran. Bullets spilled on the ground around his feet like discarded seeds. The bull was still standing where he'd left him. About twenty paces to go. He knew he had one chance at this, one chance to get his father off of those horns, hopefully alive. Walk straight up to the bull and put a bullet in his forehead. "Keep his attention on me and pray he doesn't charge."

The bull was watching him now with those crazy eyes. Jim felt his legs threatening to betray him, threatening to fold on him, to just turn away, to flee. Tears of panic clouded his eyes and he felt a whimper begin deep in his throat. He straightened out a shell from the small handful he still clutched sweaty in his hand and slid it into the chamber of the gun. Less than ten paces. Pull back on the firing pin. The clear metallic "click" told him it was cocked. Five paces. Too far. Closer. His Dad had taught him the spot to hit for a clean kill. In his mind he'd lined this creature up a hundred times. He knew exactly where he'd shoot him.

He kept moving forward, dragging his reluctant legs toward the bull. He tried to get control over his ragged breathing, tried to steady his hands. He'd have to get closer. As he slid his foot forward the bull stretched out his snout toward the rifle and began to bellow. Jim would remember that bellow later, turning it over and over in his mind. It was not the hormone-charged bawl of an enraged bull. There was something plaintive in that bellow, something lost, something at odds with the macabre scene standing before him in the barnyard.

The bull lowered his head, sniffing where Sandy's blood had dripped on the grass. As he raised it again Jim, looking down the sights on the rifle, saw the expression changing in those eyes. The crack of the .22 sounded so small, swallowed up in the bull's broad forehead, in the green hard earth of the barnyard and in the folds of the grey, layered sky. When the report of the rifle had fled, when it was spent and all its terrible damage done, the bull was still standing in front of Jim, stock still, head half raised, looking at him. There was a look in those eyes that for the first time, Jim could read. He knew. The little bull understood too late what Jim would do to him. Then the bull's legs buckled and he went down.

Peter had been between his house and the barn when he heard

the bawling of the bull and saw young Jim at a dead run, making for the tool shed. Peter's farm sat next to Sandy's. His land, like Sandy's, began at the shore of the Bras d'Or Lake and ran back from there over the "dry intervale," the level, rich land, so rare in this part of the country, back to the hillside pastures and onward up over the wooded mountain to the rear boundary, a mile and a quarter from the shore. Peter's house and barnyard sat on higher ground than Sandy's and he enjoyed a bird's-eye view of his cousin's comings and goings.

He'd thought that Jim was running from the bull, that the bull was chasing him and that he would corner poor Jim in the tool shed among the saw horses, the tools, the heavy load sleigh, the archaic riding sleigh, the cans and buckets of bolts and fittings, the engine block from Sandy's old Pontiac and the random pieces of broken implements that Sandy had gathered over the years and that now lay, leaned and hung in their many and varied poses awaiting with infinite patience the ministrations that would see them whole.

Peter, envisioning young Jim entrapped among that ordered mayhem, had jumped in the truck and headed for his cousin's barnyard. He reached the gate to the barnyard just in time to hear the report of the rifle. Jim's back hid most of what was going on but there was no mistaking Jim's stance and the sound of the gun. He'd watched Jim's frantic attempt with those sweaty trembling fingers to jam another greasy bullet into the gun. "He needn't have bothered," Peter would say later. "As it was, the bull was dead standing there."

Peter was not unaware of his role as chronicler of the drama that had unfolded in the barnyard. In the two weeks since "the accident" he had been called upon many times to tell the story, sitting in his own kitchen and more often in Sandy's kitchen as neighbours arrived loaded down with food, concern and curiosity. They sat by turns in the kitchen during that spell when Sandy was still in the hospital, listening, exclaiming at the treachery of that bull and bulls in general. They marvelled at the bravery of young Jim and the fortitude of Poor Sandy, as he was now referred to, in surviving at all such a brutal and treacherous attack. Peter, as taciturn as he could be at times, enjoyed a good story. He enjoyed even more telling a good story and this after all was a dandy. It was a story that would outlive them all.

But Peter only knew part of the story. Jim knew the whole story and so did his dad. He should have kept that bull away or at least been there to warn his father, but he didn't do either. He'd gotten scared and he'd let the bull get in. He knew it and his father knew it too, and today his father had gotten home from the hospital while Jim was in school. Now was the time for truth, the truth he couldn't acknowledge in front of anyone, not even his father, not in the stark, crowded strangeness of that hospital room.

All his life this room, his parents' bedroom, had been at once a refuge and a foreign place. His eyes searched from the low wooden chair in the corner, to the clothes hanging on pegs on the wall facing the foot of the bed, to the window with its shining white paint framing the age-wavered glass and then, avoiding looking at his father again, Jim let his eyes drop, tracing the clean black lines between the tiles and then the broken, jagged cracks that ran the length of the room following the joints between the spruce floorboards underneath. The boards had worn unevenly over the years between the time when his grandfather had laid them and the time his father had covered them with the new tiles that now betrayed his best efforts.

Perhaps it was because of his father lying there, looking in his sleep like a child that had grown old before his time, or perhaps it was because Jim knew that when he finished school that year, he was leaving. Today the room looked so small, so tenuous and fragile, unlikely as the flowered wallpaper that clung to the walls, held there against all odds by the glue that his mother had made from flour and water.

For two weeks, Jim had waited for someone to challenge him, to demand to know why he had failed to protect his father. In his head, he had gone over his defence many times. He could even hear the angry, defensive tone of his delivery. Now, standing beside his father's bed, seeing his father sleeping, his face grey against the whiteness of the pillows, Jim's defences fled.

"Dad, I'm sorry," he said. The last word welled up, sucking and rolling out of him in a sob like a wave breaking against the gravel beach. "I let the bull in.... I went to get the axe in the tool shed..... I was...I was scared."

Sandy, lying in his own bed for the first time in weeks, had been amazed many times over that day, amazed at his fatigue after the long drive home from the hospital, amazed at the miraculous luxury of lying in his own bed with the too-many quilts and the multitude of pillows, at the wonders of the smells coming from the kitchen, at the quiet, careful generosity of his neighbours. And then there was Margaret. Margaret coming often to the bedroom to ask if there was anything he needed. Margaret sitting gingerly on the side of the bed, straightening his pillow, touching his hair. Margaret looking at him with that look in her eyes that he hadn't seen in years. Or perhaps it was him that hadn't noticed.

Yes, it had been a day filled with wonders but none of these hit him like the wonder of his son, now standing before him shaking with the effort to swallow his sobs.

"Jim," he said. "Jim, slow down. It's not your fault." Sandy gestured toward the door with his good arm. "Close that."

"Jim, it was my own fault. You know that's true and I know it's true. Hell, the whole countryside knows that's true. It was my own damn fault."

As weak as his voice was, he dropped it even lower and beckoned to Jim to lean in close.

"Listen, Jim," he said. "It's not every day that I get this kind of treatment now, is it?"

"I guess not," said Jim, swallowing a nervous laugh that threatened to betray him.

"And more important," said Sandy, "it's not every household in the country that can claim a bona fide hero in the family, is it?"

Jim looked his father fully in the eyes for the first time since he'd awakened.

"Look, Jim, what do you say we both just enjoy it?"

Clive Doucet

The Gaelic Ship

IN 1932, MY FATHER FERN was sent to work at the presbytery in Broad Cove Chapel. He was twelve. The priest had no family and, having many other responsibilities, could not take care of the household by himself. There was a woman engaged to cook and keep the presbytery for the priest. A hired man came to do the heavy work and there was a boy who roomed at the presbytery for the light work—to keep the kitchen woodbox stocked, wash up dishes and assist the priest to serve early morning Mass.

It was a position much desired by parents, as their boys came home better educated and more confident of their future than those who did not have the same chance. My grandmother would have preferred if her sons could have gone to stay with Father DeCoste in our own village. Father DeCoste was known as a fine teacher and was able to teach both the piano and organ; but my grandparents could not secure a position there, for Father DeCoste preferred to choose a boy recommended to him from another village and in this way avoided any accusations of favouritism in his own. Other priests did the same.

In this way a position was secured for my father at Broad Cove Chapel which was about twenty-five miles southwest along the coast.

Father Archie spoke not a word of French and in the presbytery preferred Gaelic to English. Mrs. McIsaac, the woman who kept Father Archie's house, was also a Gaelic speaker and spoke English only when circumstances obliged. Today, it is such a short trip from the village of Grand Étang to Broad Cove, about forty-five minutes depending on how you drive, but in the 1930s it was four hours by horse-drawn wagon, and in winter the road was often impassable.

The Margaree Harbour bridge marks the line between the Acadian villages that spoke French and villages that spoke English and Gaelic. When Dad arrived in Broad Cove, he would have been conscious of his difference from the first second he entered the presbytery and shook hands with the priest. I'm guessing he hardly understood a word. Father Archie spoke English with a heavy Gaelic accent. What little English Dad spoke sounded more like French. The first weeks at school must have been mostly incomprehensible, made bearable by another boy who was equally miserable.

The other boy was named Neil McNeil. Fern and Neil must have been little islands of silence in the schoolyard, not able to talk to anyone else nor to each other. They could not even say their names in a way others could repeat. Was that when Dad's name began to shift from Fernand to Fern? Or Neil became known as a fighter? I don't know but I do know they became fast friends, sitting next to each other in school and looking out for each other in the schoolyard.

Neil's family were Gaelic speakers. He had red-tinged hair. His shoulders were already broad and strong beyond his years and it was clear he was going to be tall like his older brothers—but, unlike his brothers, he didn't take to English at all. His mother who spoke English had died when he was born and he had been raised mostly by his grandparents on their mountain farm. The grandparents couldn't be bothered speaking English to him, so he had learned very little.

Neil had a naturally slow, careful way about him, and he quickly became—like other country children with strong Gaelic accents— the butt of jokes, as they were regarded as hicks by the more worldly boys and girls of Broad Cove. The jokes did not inspire him to learn English; instead he became taciturn with his classmates and rarely talked unless he was forced to by the teacher. My father became a translator for Neil and did his best to protect him from the slights of their classmates.

It was difficult for Neil from the beginning. He made it clear he did not want to be at school and did not want to speak English—

regarding the language as an ugly affront. This led to many conflicts with the teacher and his classmates, some of whom grew afraid of his glowering looks, fists and temper.

On stormy nights, Neil would stay at the rectory where he was a great favourite. Mrs. McIsaac was very fond of him and called the teacher an English savage which pleased Neil, although it wasn't quite accurate as the teacher was a young McLeod whose own English was also burred with the "old language," as they called it.

Wednesday night was a card night and Mrs. McIsaac had friends visit. They all ganged round the kitchen table to play and the language of the game was the old language. Here, Neil McNeil became a different boy; instead of solemn and watchful, his face was animated and flushed, his bright blue eyes sparkling. Here, he talked a great deal. None of it my father understood, but it frequently sent the ladies into gales of laughter. Mrs. McIsaac said Neil could tell a story like his grandfather, who was known to be a great storyteller as well as "a fine figure of a man."

While the ladies played cards and Neil entertained them, my father did his homework and then did Neil's. At the end of the night he gave the completed homework to Neil explaining what he had done and why. Immediately, Neil's face grew grave as he tried to understand.

One Friday night, my father climbed the long track with Neil and his older sister to their homestead. The older sister had thick waves of auburn hair and bright blue eyes like Neil, and my father found her exceedingly pretty. From the doorway of their house, which was high on the mountain, they could see the entire sweep of Broad Cove all the way to the town of Inverness and then back up north towards his own village beneath the mountains.

Neil's sister asked him sympathetically how he was liking school. Dad blushed under her frank gaze. He was doing well but said nothing more than "okay" because he did not want to embarrass Neil who was not. "Do the girls tease you?" she asked. "I've heard that they do." He shook his head because they teased Neil more, parodying his accent and his odd Gaelic phrasing in English.

"Neil doesn't like school much," said his sister and sighed a little. "He can't seem to get the hang of English." She shrugged. "There's nothing much to it really. I used to practice in front of the mirror. You make a different face when you speak English," and she twisted her face up. "When you think your face looks like the back end of a hen, then you know you're speaking English." Fern laughed.

Neil's grandparents appeared and the girl went upstairs to her own room. Neil and Fern went out to catch the cows for milking. With his grandparents, Neil spoke only Gaelic and my father did not understand a word until supper, when Neil's sister joined them and translated for him as they talked.

Neil's father was away in the woods working for Bowater with a team of horses, leaving only a two-year-old colt, the house being ready for winter with the food put up and the barn stuffed with hay. The evening ended in laughter with Neil's grandfather telling some stories. Neil did the translations, but they weren't translations, they were different stories filled with bawdy illusions which set the old people laughing even more than the original, and their merriment infected everyone else.

At Thanksgiving, Neil failed his tests and as the Christmas exams approached Father Archie began to sit with Neil, coaching him in a mixture of Gaelic and English. It was then that Neil started to learn how to read! He had memorized the alphabet in a straight line from A to Z but could not recognize the letters when they were out of order. Father Archie figured this out and taught him how to recognize them when they were in words.

Neil learned to read very quickly—although Neil said afterwards that it wasn't Father Archie who taught him. It was Mrs. McIsaac. She taught him how to use the alphabet to read Gaelic and once he understood how to read Gaelic, he figured English too.

One day, at the back of the schoolyard, some bigger boys circled my father demanding that he say "three" because at that time he could not make the H sound, dropping it and saying "tree." When he could not make the sound correctly, they began to punch him. Neil came round the corner of the schoolhouse, howled a Gaelic war cry and charged the boys, proceeding in a few seconds to bloody the nose of one, blacken the eye of another, and rip the shirt of a third.

When all five boys appeared in school with banged-up faces and torn clothes, the teacher was told it was Neil McNeil's fault and the "French kid."

That night, McLeod the teacher came to the rectory, and he did not waste a minute before crossing swords with Father Archie. The whole house could hear him. "Do you think I like it? But I canna teach in the old language. Gaelic is dead! Dead as a doornail. Do you think they speak Gaelic in Ottawa? Do you think they speak Gaelic in Montreal? There's no future for the old language! You know that as well as I do."

Father Archie said something quietly that no one but the teacher heard.

"Do you think Neil is going to live on a mountainside for the rest of his life?"

Father Archie—who in spite of his size was a very mild-mannered man—again said something in reply that no one else could hear.

"You're not helping me, Father Archie, nor is Mrs. McIsaac. His brothers learned English. His sister is one of my best students. You must be giving the boy the illusion that there's some future in the old language because that's all it is, an illusion."

"McLeod, you'll not be yelling at me in me own house," said Father Archie now, loud enough for others to hear.

"For sure, I'm sorry, Father, but there's a reason Gaelic is not allowed in the school. It's not as if I haven't thought about it. How do you expect Neil McNeil to learn English if he is always speaking Gaelic?" And he looked hard at Father Archie, "Are you speaking Gaelic with him?"

Father Archie looked uncomfortable and did not reply. The teacher continued. "And what about the Doucet boy fighting? Your boy is supposed to set an example for the others. What kind of example is fighting?"

"His marks are fine."

"That's not the point."

"Boys will be boys," shrugged Father Archie. "I seem to remember you getting into a few scrapes and I don't remember yelling at you for it."

This time it was young McLeod's turn to look embarrassed, and they left it at that.

At school, Neil McNeil and Fern Doucet were separated, with Neil on one side of the class and my father on the other. On Wednesdays Neil was prohibited from playing cards with Mrs. McIsaac. He did homework with Father Archie and they tried not to speak Gaelic.

Christmas approached and Neil was allowed to go back to the storytelling group which began as soon as more tea was made and the card game finished. Then, it was Neil McNeil and Black Donald McIsaac who were the stars, both having the knack of telling stories. The *Brenagh* sailed in on one of those evenings.

"Not so long ago, there was a ship that sailed out of North Sydney captained by Angus Joe MacDonald, who crewed his ship entirely with Gaelic speakers. Captain Angus didn't much care if a man had ever been on a ship before, because he figured sailing could be taught, but he cared about Gaelic, for once you had crossed the bridge of the *Brenagh* the only songs were Gaelic, the only stories were Gaelic, the only language was Gaelic. It was as if you were in a Gaelic country.

"On the *Brenagh*, the English language was never heard.

"Captain Angus Joe was the last captain of the last Gaelic ship in all of Nova Scotia. The captain's wife and children travelled with him, which was the custom in those days. The *Brenagh* was known as a lucky ship and there were many who would have liked to sail with the Captain if they'd had the old language. Captain Angus Joe sailed the *Brenagh* from one end of the globe to the other, from China to Africa, Africa to South America, and back again. There was no port he didn't know or wasn't welcome. They say the *Brenagh* never lost a cargo nor hailed a bad harbour. The Captain always had a line-up of men wanting to sail with him. They came from all

The Gaelic Ship

over—Brittany, Wales, Ireland, Scotland, Nova Scotia—everywhere there were Gaelic speakers.

"Now one day his wife put her foot down and he had to stop sailing. The *Brenagh* went up for sale and she went quickly for a good price, being known as a lucky ship.

"Now here's the queer part. Captain Angus tried to sell her to a Gaelic-speaking Captain but could find no one that suited his fancy. Instead she went to an English Captain who had coveted her for a long time. But the new Captain and his English crew foundered off Madagascar, losing all hands on her first voyage—and that was the end of the *Brenagh*."

"Why did the Captain quit?" asked Neil.

"It was the wife. When they had the fourth child, she didn't want them to be sailing anymore. But here is the interesting thing: they say the Captain's oldest boy is putting together a sealing crew in North Sydney this winter with nothing but Gaelic speakers, just like his father used to do. Won't that be something? Make a little money and do it in the old language."

This story was Neil McNeil's favourite and he was always pestering for more stories of the *Brenagh*. Black Donald obliged him, the *Brenagh* having sailed in many strange places and having had many great adventures. She had even run into Captain Joshua Slocum, the first man to sail around the world alone.

Normally, the spring seal hunt is far out in the Gulf. The pack ice sweeps down from the north, and somewhere between Newfoundland and the Magdalen Islands millions of pups are born on the ice, safe from any predators until they're ready to swim back home. It happens only rarely that the big herds come as far as Cape Breton, but in March of 1935 the ice was exceptionally strong and it packed up against the shoreline in a vast field along the entire coast. The men began to leave the villages to walk across the ice to join the men from the ships in the hunt which was taking place at the edge of the ice in clear view of the shore.

Neil McNeil decided he would go too, just to watch, and he

asked my father Fern to go along. Now my father was from a fishing village and he knew fishing seals is not as easy as it looks. The winds can shift and suddenly the ice begins to break up and you're in trouble caught between the floes and open water with nowhere to go. It's nervous work. You always have to have one eye on the wind and one eye on the ice, watching in case it should begin to shift and break up. But this Saturday was especially beautiful. The sun was warm and the ice white and perfectly flat, stretching towards the horizon.

My father and Neil stood on the ice looking out. The ice looked as solid and secure as the day is long and they thought they could see the sealers further up the coast towards my father's village of Grand Étang. "I bet we could walk straight to Grand Étang and be back in time for supper," said Neil. And suddenly my father had a great longing to go home.

"Maybe we can find the Gaelic ship," said Neil, looking not toward the headland which marked the village of Grand Étang but further north towards the dark smoke smudge on the horizon which marked the hunt. The day was perfect, sunny and clear with the ice so smooth and so tempting to walk on that the boys began to gambol across it like young colts let out from the winter barn into a spring pasture. In no time at all, they were passing the mouth of Margaree Harbour, moving quickly in a dead straight line for Grand Étang. In the distance, they saw a sealing ship steaming northwards towards the herd, but the herd and the sealers themselves got no closer.

They were able to move quickly over the hard ice, running as fast as their legs would take them—much easier on the hard-packed snow than on the road, which was deeply rutted, holed and broken up. Soon, they had gone so far that it was easier to just keep going than to return. When the boys walked in the kitchen door in Grand Étang, Dad's mother did not know whether to be angry or happy to see her son home, and after some chiding about walking on the ice, decided on being happy. She served them a grand meal which they fell upon, and then just as promptly fell sound asleep, sitting straight up in the kitchen rocking chairs. They awoke to find themselves in the middle of an Acadian party with fiddle music, food and lots of neighbours who had dropped in to welcome the prodigal son.

When Neil McNeil recognized a tune, he would sing in Gaelic with a fine, clear voice—the others just listening.

In the evening, my uncle Dennis hitched grandfather's fastest mare to the cutter and drove them back over the ice directly to Broad Cove. Dennis was not a great talker and they said little, but that trip under the stars—the sled's runners making nothing but the crisp, bright sounds of sharp sliding as they flew along—was engraved in my father's memory.

On Sunday, the whole village of Broad Cove knew the boys had walked over the ice to Grand Étang, and it conferred a certain notoriety on them both. On Monday, they received their Easter marks. After school, my father found Neil sitting on the small dock below the presbytery, gazing out to sea. "I want to go to sealing on the *Brenagh*," he said, "and never hear English again."

My father nodded, understanding.

"In your village, can you speak French in school?"

"The teachers teach in French, but a lot of the books are English."

"But speaking French wouldn't be forbidden?"

"No. We speak French."

"You can speak it in the schoolyard?"

"Yes."

"So why can't we speak Gaelic in Broad Cove? The teacher speaks Gaelic to Mrs. McIsaac, but he won't let me speak Gaelic. What is wrong with our language?" Neil McNeil said this slowly as if it was costing him a lot to form the words.

My father did not know what to say and so he just shrugged. He knew that he was lucky. He did not have to stay in Broad Cove. One day, he could go home.

On Thursday, Neil McNeil was not at school. He had been at the presbytery the night before, but my father did not see him in the morning because he had served early morning Mass with Father

Archie. It wasn't until noon that he realized Neil was not in school. He went to ask the teacher where he might find him. The teacher did not know.

My father walked straight down to the shore. He thought that he could see a small dot, far out to sea, moving steadily towards the north. He went directly to Father Archie and said he thought Neil McNeil had gone looking for the Gaelic ship.

Neil McNeil's father came down from the mountain with horses and sleighs, carrying Neil's older brothers and neighbours. It was a McNeil clan gathering. Neil's father was a tall, thin man with a hawk face who said nothing and no one said anything to him, so dark and grim did he look. He stood for a long time on the shore looking for any sign of his son. One of Neil's brothers said he thought he could see something. Suddenly with a Gaelic war cry that seemed to rise from the bottom of the earth, the men left, the horses galloping towards the horizon across the vast, white plain.

Later, it began to snow and snow, great white flakes, and it was warm and the snow slowed their progress and it began to be hard to see. The men did not stop, even when they could not see. Neil McNeil's father drove the horses all the way north to Bay St. Lawrence where the ice ended. They lost his best horse where the ice suddenly became soft and separated under him. The animal floundered down into the frigid waters. He was the strongest, fastest horse that Neil's father owned. His great violet eyes were shrinking into the white with fear as he thrashed and struggled to get back on the ice, but kept slipping back. The men became soaked and frozen trying to cut the terrified animal free from the sleigh, but could not do it.

It was five days before the men came home—worn out and half frozen.

They had found no one who had met a Gaelic-speaking boy and they never found a Gaelic ship, just inshore sealers and a couple of English-speaking crews out of Sydney and St. John's.

Maureen Hull

Finches

ALANA'S HUSBAND BRAD WORKED IN A BAR in downtown Halifax four nights a week. He had been going to St. Mary's, studying commerce, but by the end of October he'd given that up. It was his third try, and she didn't think—no matter how persuasive he was—the registrar would let him in again.

Screw the tuition, he said. He made a lot more working the bar than she made pinning and sewing costumes at the theatre so what could she say? She hoped he'd finally figure it out. Whatever it was he was going to do.

In mid-November he came home at 3 a.m. with two finches in a cage. A man had left them on the copper-topped bar. He said his girlfriend had thrown him out and he had nowhere to keep them warm anymore. He was living in his car, and he was leaving the next morning for Montreal.

There was a male and a female. The male was noisy and sociable, even in the middle of the night. Guy's a speed freak, Brad said. Grey on his back and wings, white on his belly, with red patches on his head. He drank water from the cup Alana refilled—it had spilled on the cage floor on the drive home—and then flew to the top bar and sang, pouring out notes in a grand, reckless rush. Alana was charmed.

What's his name? she asked, but Brad couldn't remember. She named him Nathaniel.

The female was brown all over and skittish. Martha, said Brad. They covered the cage with a bath towel and went to bed.

When she got home each night from work, Nathaniel sang to her. She made supper to his music. It lightened the air; it lifted her spirits. She wasn't sure what Brad did all day. Probably what he'd always done—went for coffee, met his friends, played handball, scored a little weed. Some of the friends came home with him for dinner on the nights he didn't work. Brad made them do dishes afterwards. He'd wave a dishtowel around, directing, drying a plate or two. His male friends flirted with her, and his female friends flirted with him. The air was silly with it. Everyone laughed a lot and drank red wine and Tenpenny ale.

Nathaniel was building a nest. When she discovered him ripping up the paper on the cage bottom and trying to shape it, Alana bought him a box of nesting material and wired it to the inside of the cage. He was so excited his songs tripped all over themselves. He pulled beakfuls out and began to arrange them on the cage floor. Periodically, he'd stop and pester Martha. Sex lasted only a few seconds, a whirring, feathered affair. Then he'd fly to the top bar and sing about how fantastic he was, how grand life was. Martha looked put upon.

While Nathaniel was up on the side of the cage, yanking out fresh material, Martha was down below, kicking the nest to pieces. This went on for a day and a half, Nathaniel building, Martha destroying. See how long it takes him to notice, said Brad. When he finally caught her at it he squawked and screeched, he beat her with his wings, he chased her around the cage. Alana, who hadn't particularly warmed to Martha, was upset. First he'd raped Martha, then when she didn't want kids, he beat her. Alana wanted to separate them, put Nathaniel in a smaller cage. A very small cage. Teach him a lesson.

Leave them alone, said Brad. It's normal, it's natural. She'll settle down.

Shut up, Alana said to Nathaniel when he began to whistle and sing. Just shut up. Eventually Martha laid an egg on the cage floor, far from Nathaniel's nest. It lay there for a few days while both birds ignored it. Alana put it in an eggcup, on the top shelf of her spice rack.

Brad got a new job, out on the oil rigs. What do you do out

there? she asked. Whatever they want, he said. The boss likes me, he's training me. I can make big money. When he came home the hall closet was filled with his gear. Huge boots and coveralls and whatnot. He was gone three weeks, then home one. He spent most of the week at a cottage in Hubbards a couple of his friends had bought. Alana worked six days a week, so she went out Saturday night and came back on Sunday. They were all there, all the boys and girls, and all of them partying hard. At some point an argument would get out of hand. A girl would break down and weep on Alana's shoulder. Threaten to drown herself in the lake. Alana got fed up with being the sympathetic one. Some weekends she didn't go.

Martha was dead on the cage floor. Brad was home; he lifted her out and wrapped her in newspaper and put her in the garbage. They watched Nathaniel for a few days, and he was definitely not as bright and cheerful. Lonesome, they decided.

They skipped the mall shops and went to a pet store on the corner of Queen and Morris. A woman with an untidy grey bun and a burgundy smock was hauling sacks of bird seed from the back. Brad gave her a hand and Alana walked down an aisle of cages, trying to decide.

Surrounded by flying jewels, whirring and whistling, Alana chose a saucy pair, smaller than the others, but so lively they seemed to bounce. Australian zebra finches. Brad bought a bigger cage, more birdseed and a cuttlebone. They need calcium, the woman said, this is the head bone of a cuttlefish. Alana had a vague notion of what a cuttlefish was. Like a sort of octopus, she whispered to Brad. We should have got a third one, said Brad when they got home. Nathaniel needs a lady friend, we weren't thinking.

The three finches scattered seed and water. They were messy creatures, but Alana forgave them because of the music. Sometimes, at night, it was a relief to put the towel over the cage and have a little quiet.

The Merchant of Venice opened and Alana had a week off before they began production on *The Collected Works of Billy the Kid*. After velvet doublets, sweeping capes and plumed hats, dressing a few cowboys was going to be easy. She drove down to Shelburne to see her high school best friend. They'd run into each other a month earlier on Barrington Street. Come and visit, Julie'd said. Stay a few days. Brad was offshore. Alana gave a key to Syl from the box office, who was fighting with his boyfriend and needed a place to stay for a few days. Syl would feed the birds. She hoped their music would cheer him up. He looked like hell.

Julie and Leo had a house on the ocean with stained-glass windows in the halls, a large wainscotted dining room, and a panelled library. There was a small sewing room for Julie and a study for Leo. What a great place to have kids, Alana said.

They went for walks along the rocky shore. There's a sandy beach just up the road, said Julie, but I'd rather walk on the rocks. It was too late to swim. Julie didn't have a job, there was too much to do to the house and in the spring, the garden. She volunteered at the library and taught a watercolour class, one day a week at Sunny Haven for Seniors. Leo was a dentist, and fifteen years older. He had grey in his mustache. Alana didn't know how to talk to him. You must be so happy here, said Alana.

I am, I love it here. Julie began to cry. He's in love with someone else, she said. I had a miscarriage last summer and then he decided he didn't want kids, and now his bitch of a girlfriend's pregnant and he's changed his mind again and I'm going to lose this house. Because he's leaving and I can't afford to keep it by myself. I could forgive him, we could make it work. I really wanted to sleep with Gerry last winter and I didn't because I was married. The asshole. The jerk.

Alana drove back the next morning. She wondered if Brad was sleeping with anyone. Once, she'd thought Kim, but Kim had a new boyfriend. They came to dinner a couple of times and were crazy in love. Brad had rolled his eyes. Not Kim, then.

Alana had begun a flirtation with an actor. They had lunches together, in quiet little basement bars. They kissed, deeply, dangerously. As if they were heading for a cliff. It was exciting. A cowboy, he wore his boots all over town. She loved the way he smelled: leather, and a little fresh sweat. Brad's clothes smelled like metal and oil. Even after he showered, a faint trace lingered. The cowboy's wife came to town for opening night and there was an end to it. Alana was relieved. They were getting too close to the cliff edge, and she didn't want to fall off, she just wanted to almost fall off.

One of the zebras looked unwell. Sluggish, and hunched. Rhianon and St. Michael, she'd named them. Rhianon flitted from perch to perch, Nathaniel flung seed all over the floor, and St. Michael stopped flying. His eyes were dull. Brad was offshore. She would have to take the bird to the vet tomorrow on her lunch hour. She cooked an egg and crumbled the yolk up with a little milk. St. Michael ignored it, Rhianon and Nathaniel scarfed it down.

Something woke her in the middle of the night. A feeling, a silence. She switched on the kitchen light and uncovered the cage. St. Michael was lying on his back, shuddering, his claws drawn up. She'd never touched the finches and she didn't know what to do. She filled a hot water bottle, wrapped it in a towel, and reached inside the cage. Her hand shook, and shook harder as it hovered over St. Michael. She didn't know why she was so terrified. She picked him up, her hand rattling around at the end of her arm, she was going to drop him. Her whole body shook and shook as she laid him on the towel. She laid a facecloth over him, to keep the heat in and propped the end of it over a teacup to make a tent so he could breathe. Nathaniel chirped and scolded. Alana cried so hard and so fiercely that she folded up and sank to the floor. She wrapped her nightgown around her legs and sobbed into her knees.

The Saturday before, she and her friend Amy and Amy's three-year-old son Todd had set off for a winter picnic. Cheesecake and ham sandwiches and thermoses of soup and crusty bread. The roads had been slippery, and it started to sleet as they drove from the city. Everything got nasty, and they pulled off to the side and wondered if it would stop and why the weatherman had proved so unreliable.

She turned the car around and they crept back to the city, avoiding a truck and two cars that had skidded off and sat half in the ditch, half on the road.

Alana was worried about Todd, that he would be disappointed, and that he would fuss. Amy spread a blanket on Alana's living room rug and they ate their picnic on the floor and stared in wonder at the howling storm outside. Todd drew pictures of transformers on every scrap of paper Alana could find and then he fell asleep. They're not so hard, said Amy. They just take up a lot of your time. You have to be thinking ahead, to what will occupy them next. Alana didn't know how she did it. She was sure she couldn't. She couldn't lift a sick bird out of a cage without falling to pieces. She could never have children.

Find someone to take the finches, she told Brad, when he came back. I'm going to Cape Breton for the weekend. She'd buried St. Michael in St. Paul's Cemetery. Chopped up the semi-frozen dirt under a bush with a hatchet she'd borrowed from props. When she came back from visiting her folks, Brad was at the cottage in Hubbards. The lake was frozen, everyone was skating and drinking hot buttered rum. She'd go in the morning, take some lasagne and some beer. She wished things were over. She wished she lived somewhere else. She wished she had the nerve to do what she wanted.

Months later, at the opening night party for *Waiting for Godot,* she met the man who had taken the finches. How are they doing? she asked.

I got them for my teenagers, he said, for when they come to visit me. My daughter wants to be a veterinarian, and my son, he keeps pigeons, you know, the homing kind. When the little guy started to build a nest they got all excited. Did a bunch of research. They fed them chopped egg and bugs and god knows what all else. Halibut liver oil or something. They left detailed instructions on the fridge: how much to feed them, and when. Baby jars of made-up food. And their cell numbers, in big black numbers in case of emergency. Like I don't know them by heart. I followed the instructions like my life depended on it. I didn't want to be the one to screw it up. The little one, Rhianon, she laid four eggs.

Nathaniel must have been happy, she said.

He was over the moon, and then they hatched and there was such squawking and fussing. They drove those parents hard, always wanting to be fed. And then there were four baby finches trying to learn to fly. I had to buy a really big cage. It was a circus, I'll tell you. My kids, they can't wait to get to my place, to check up on their babies. I'm a bird grandpa.

The man's laughter pulled Alana right out of herself. She couldn't stop smiling.

D.C. Troicuk

Sin

"You'll never guess who was in the store today," Dad said. "Tom Grant."

He was talking to Mother in his quiet voice, same as me and Riley talk when there's other people around and we're saying stuff nobody's s'posed to know but us. Me and Riley are brothers.

"Bought one of those new transistor radios," Dad said. "Runs on batteries."

Dodie's quiet voice was louder than anybody's. "Funny he didn't buy two," she said. Dodie is Grampa's lady friend.

Riley spat out corn niblets in a hurry to get his question out before somebody else did. "Why would he buy two?"

We saw the warning on Mother's face but I guess Dad didn't because he gave him an answer anyway. "Seems he's got two of everything else."

Mother twinkled her eyes at Dad and passed him the mashed potatoes. She was trying not to laugh. Me and Riley kicked each other under the table like we knew what was so funny. But we didn't, really. We just knew, whatever it was, Dodie didn't like it.

Dodie started coming up from Port Hawkesbury to see Grampa after Nanny went into the nursing home. But she'd stay over with us, not with him. To keep up appearances, Dad said. Because Dodie is a holy roller. She used to know Nanny too, but the day she went to visit, Nanny kept asking me who the woman in the hall with Grampa was. Nanny doesn't remember me and Riley all the time either. She'll call me Robbie—that's our uncle who lives in Truro. And she'll call Riley Gordie—that's our Dad.

The first time Grampa brought Dodie to our house she latched onto Mother. "Like we were bosom buddies," Mother told Dad that night. Mother hardly ever says if she doesn't like somebody but Riley tried like heck to find out if she really liked Dodie. He'd say, "Is Dodie ever—" And then he'd just pick a word. *Ugly. Lazy. Nuts.* Or else he'd say something we heard Dad say, even if we didn't know what it meant. *Melodramic. Fitiful. Exasperative.* Anything to get Mother going, 'cause when you get her going that's when she says the really good stuff we aren't s'posed to know.

But the only thing she says about Dodie is: "If you can't say anything nice about somebody...."

And me and Riley got to say: "Don't say anything at all."

Dodie must know Mr. Grant because she made a face every time Dad said his name.

"If Mr. Grant is Dad's friend," Riley said, "how come we don't know him?"

Mother touched her chin. That's her signal for us not to talk with our mouth full. "They just went to school together. That's different from being friends," she said. "He was here once. Remember that nice man who drove your father home the night of the hurricane?"

"Oh, yeah," Riley said.

I remembered him too. Riley and me hung over the bannister on the landing trying to get a look at the two drownded rats Mother let in, Dad and this other man getting out of their soaking overcoats and drying their hair with Mother's good towels. There was a kind of excitement in the air, and they laughed and clapped each other on the back like they just made a narrow escape from Alcatraz or somewheres, like in the movies.

Everybody went into the kitchen for hot toddies and Riley and me snuck down to the dining room and made camp in the dark under the table. We twisted our arms and legs around the legs of the table and chairs and listened through the half-open door. Mr. Grant talked about how he was laid off and how he had two married daughters who lived in Halifax, and about his garden. He grew apples and all kinds of vege'bles, but it was the worst year he ever saw for potato bugs.

Mother said, "You should bring Mrs. Grant by for tea sometime. Is she a local girl?"

Things got real quiet then. Mr. Grant started making excuses why he had to go and Mother made excuses about why he should wait till the storm let up. Dad kept clearing his throat until she said, "At least change into some dry things before you go."

Riley and me thought that was kind of stupid, because he'd only be soaked again before he got to his car. Mother went upstairs to get him some of Dad's clothes, and while Mr. Grant was changing in the back bedroom there was a lot of whispering in the kitchen. Mother squealed like that time she saw a mouse and she burst out laughing. Dad tried to shush her, but Mr. Grant came back too soon. So she pretended she was trying not to laugh at us.

"What are you boys doing up? Come out from under that table and get to bed this instant."

Upstairs, Riley and me climbed onto my bunk. We pulled the covers over our heads and turned on the flashlight and tried to figure out what the heck was going on.

On Saturday Dad borrowed Grampa's truck and took us for a drive in the country.

"Where we going, Daddy?" Riley said.

"Somewhere," Dad said.

When me and Riley were little we'd get all excited when he said mysterious stuff like that. Now we know he does it on purpose just so we get excited about all the great places the road might go. But it never does. We only ever wind up someplace like the dump where he won't let us get out of the car, or a service station where we got to hang around for hours and hours and we aren't allowed to touch anything.

This time we took the road that goes to Port Morien and the sand bar. We go there all the time to dig clams. I knew if you kept going it took you to Mira. That was where the MacKenzies used to have their bungalow before they moved away. Riley was real little then.

We didn't go all the way to Mira though. We turned down this one-lane road going in through the trees. I remembered it because Mother used to say, "I wonder what could be down there." And Dad would joke around and say, "Might be Heaven," or stuff like that. But one time when I said the same thing he told me there was a farm down there. I didn't know which one was true because I couldn't see a garden or a house or anything from the road, just woods.

Me and Riley like it when we get to ride in Grampa's pickup because it only has a front seat. In our car we have to ride in the back. On the driveway the trees were real close and scraped along the doors. Dad let us roll down the window and we climbed over each other taking turns putting our faces up close and jumping back before the branches could hit us in the face. It didn't hurt. But Dad said, "Quit that before somebody loses an eye."

The truck's tires bumped down into deep holes, grass brushed the floor under our feet. There was a big splash and Riley and me thought the bottom of the truck was going to be torn off. We lifted our legs high and we were scared, but just for a second. Then we started to laugh, and we were still laughing when Dad pulled up next to a beat-up station wagon—the same one that drove Dad home in the storm. It was Mr. Grant's car.

Dad took the bag with the clothes that Mother washed and ironed for Mr. Grant and went to the door. He didn't say, "Stay in the truck," so we didn't.

This was nothing like Dad's usual stops. Riley was already swinging on a big tire hanging from a tree but I couldn't decide what to do first. I stretched and looked around the way Grampa would. There was a rake and a pile of leaves near the house, and a shed with a stack of wood piled outside it and an axe stuck in a stump, and a big barn with a door open wide. A grey cat was just going in. He stopped and looked back at me and he meowed like he was saying, "Foll-ooow." So I did.

I never saw a lady in overalls before, but there was one in the barn. They were pretty overalls with lots of flowers all over them, like somebody sewed them on. She was pretty too, with long straight yellow hair that made me think of the girls on our street who go to the high school, but the closer I came the more she reminded me of my teacher, Mrs. Peters, who has three kids older than me.

The lady said, "Pandora had kittens. Want to see?"

Pandora led the way over to a cardboard box. The kittens climbed all over each other so I couldn't even count them till they were all in a row attached to her belly. There were six. When I saw where they were attaching themselves I was glad Riley wasn't there because you never knew what he was gonna blurt out. He gets us in trouble all the time just for saying out loud what anybody can see.

"They're a week old now," the lady said. She had her hand in the box, stroking the mother cat.

"Are you Mrs. Grant?" I said.

She just smiled. "And who are you?"

"I'm Arthur."

"What are you doing here, Arthur?"

I shrugged.

"Did you come for some apples?"

I didn't know.

"Maybe you'd like a kitten, when they're a little older."

I wanted so bad to say yes. Riley would've said yes.

"Ask your Dad," she said. "See what he says."

She went to the other side of the barn where I couldn't see what she was doing. She was singing the Kumbaya song that Riley and me know from our camp-outs when Mr. Chisholm brings his guitar. I sat on the floor and petted all the fat bellies but I only picked up one of the kittens, the black-and-white one with the four white paws. I already had a really good name for him: Mittens.

When I came out of the barn Riley called me over. I had to squint up my eyes to see him. "Where'd you get that?" I said.

"Mrs. Grant gave it to me," he said, biting into the apple.

"She did not. You never even saw her."

"Did too," Riley said. "She was in the house the whole time with Dad and me."

"She was not. She was in the barn the whole time. With me."

Riley looked over at the barn like he didn't believe me. So I said, just to prove it, "She's going to give me a kitten."

"I don't think so," said Dad. Him and Mr. Grant loaded bushel baskets filled with apples onto the back of the truck. There were six altogether. Dad had trouble latching the tail gate. Mr. Grant said maybe it just needed some oil. He went to the shed and came back with a little red can with a long spout.

We wanted to watch but then I saw the lady from the barn going across the yard. I elbowed Riley hard in the ribs. "See? That's her."

She ran up the steps to the house. Another woman came out and they stood there with Mr. Grant and waved as we drove away.

"Holy cow," Riley said. "There's two Mrs. Grants."

Dad pulled hard on the parking brake to keep the truck from rolling back down our driveway.

Mother came out to meet him. "Well?" she said, smirking.

"Saw them both," Dad said under his breath.

He jerked his head toward Dodie. She was sitting in one of the wicker chairs on our verandah with her suitcases and her knitting bag and two big bags from K-Mart like she was waiting for a bus. They don't have a K-Mart in Port Hawkesbury.

"What's up?" he said. "I thought she was staying the weekend."

"Don't ask," Grampa grumbled, coming from the toolshed with his hand out for the keys.

"Look at this, Pop," Dad said. "Apples for everybody. I even got extra for Dodie's church ladies to make their pies for their fall fair. Give me a hand, would you? We'll dump them in the old potato bins in the shed for now."

"Leave ours," Grampa said. "I'm taking herself home. Then I'm going down to spend a couple of days with Robbie. You've got enough for his crew, do you?"

"Sure," Dad said, but he was scratching his head. "The thing is, Tom needs the baskets back right away." He thought for another minute. "Maybe we could lay down that new tarp and dump the apples on it?"

Grampa jabbed his finger toward the verandah, so we knew he was riled up. "Gordie," he said, "so help me God, I never gave that woman any encouragement. I tried to tell her I don't need anybody coming over to clean my house and do my laundry. I just figured she's a church-going woman doing a good deed, that's what I thought. And I let her come because she's got nobody. I feel sorry for her. That's all."

He started to walk away, but he made a circle and came right back to where he started and tapped the same finger on Dad's chest. "She knows darn well I got a wife. Half the time your mother doesn't know me from Adam, but those times when she looks at me and lights up—ah, Gordie, why would I pass that up for a trip to K-Mart with herself over there? If she wants to get in a snit over that, so be it."

Dad took a bushel to the shed for us and came back with the tarp. Riley and me climbed up into the truck bed and helped Grampa arrange Dodie's suitcases and bags and his gear box. When the tarp was down we tipped over the baskets making a bumpy red pool around our ankles.

Dodie came over and she screwed up her face. "Sour as lemons. I can tell just by looking at them."

We heard a sound like the cat hocking up a fur ball. But it was coming from Dodie. The next thing we knew she hocked up a big gob of spit right onto the apples.

Riley's mouth dropped open, and I guess mine did too. We stared at the white foam of her spit. Mother and Dad stared at Dodie.

Grampa plucked out a handful of slimy apples and fired them one after another into the neighbour's wood lot.

"Get in the truck, Dodie," he said.

He headed for the house, holding his hands away from him, the way Riley and me did after that time we tried to get our baseball out of the bucket of whitewash.

Mother pointed after him. "Boys, go wash up for supper."

We went after Grampa but when we got around the front of our car Riley yanked me down to the ground. We crouched there for a minute, then we sneaked back along the other side of the driveway where the bank was steep and the shadows were dark. We lay down flat in the bushes to hear what Mother and Dad were going to say to Dodie, but they must have gone to the house too because she was alone behind the truck, fiddling with something.

The tailgate creaked. All of a sudden there was a kind of thunder and we jumped up just in time to see the apples running like a red river down the grooves of our driveway all the way to the road. Down on the pavement there was a screech of tires, and a loud crash.

Riley and me raced after them. There wasn't much to see. Mr. Shearing's car was in the ditch, that was all. The fender was dented pretty good, though, and Mr. Shearing was cursing and mad as heck.

Everybody hung around till after the tow-truck left. When we came back up the driveway Grampa and Dad tried to figure out how the tailgate came undone.

Dodie was staring at us. "You really should keep a better eye on those boys, June."

Mother gasped. "What are you suggesting?"

I only ever heard Mother use that tone when she was ready to throttle us. Dodie opened her mouth like she had an answer but before she could get a word out Grampa told her again, "Get in the truck, Dodie."

Supper was late that night. Riley was quiet. I can always tell when he's thinking things over real hard. All of a sudden he turned to Dad. "Is bigamy a sin?"

Mother dropped her fork on the floor. "Where on earth did you hear a word like that?"

"From Dodie. She told Grampa that's what Mr. Grant is doing."

"Dodie doesn't know what she's talking about," Mother said. "There is only one Mrs. Grant."

Riley frowned. "Then who's the other one?"

Mother looked to Dad like she needed help and Dad waved his hand like he was patting the air. That's his signal for us to calm down, but this time he was doing it for her. He said to Riley, "Did Dodie happen to say what bigamy is?"

"No. But she said it's a sin," Riley said. "Grampa told her it's not. He said in the Bible they all did it."

"Did 'it'?" Dad challenged. "Did what, Riley? What did they do?"

I slunk down in my chair. Even if I knew, I wouldn't've said. Because everybody was using their tones today, the ones where no matter what you said you were in for it.

It got so quiet I could hear everybody chew. Then Dad started talking, the way he did sometimes when nobody else had anything to say. "You know what's a sin?" he said. "Knowing people are starving all over the world and you just throw good food away. That's one kind of sin. Putting people down for living their own lives, when they're not bothering anybody. That's another kind. Blaming somebody for something you did yourself. Those are all sins, if you ask me."

He never said a word about Dodie or apples or Mr. and Mrs. and Mrs. Grant. He didn't have to. Riley and me are pretty much starting to figure it out for ourselves.

Dave Doucette

Carving Initials

DIRT DOESN'T DO MUCH TALKING about its footprints or bicycle tracks. It hangs on to their impressions a bit, but we never know much about who went by. And when it rains, it's all over.

Tommy's bike was stolen from under the step last Tuesday. The thief came at night. Four days now and not a clue. No one saw anything. But there was no sense of worrying about it anymore. It was gone and it was time to forget it. Tommy walked down into the woods instead, to the Sunny Spot. It was summer now and the sun would be nice there. Maybe, if he had put his name on the bike—but everyone knew it. What was the difference? It was a good bike too.

At the Sunny Spot, Tommy lay down where the ground was dry. Steam was coming out of the ground and hanging in around the tree roots. It was rising and disappearing, like little snakes. In the branches, above the steam, laughs were coming out of the leaves. And even farther above, all the way up to the sky, figures and bodies were in the clouds. They went by like houses. Under Tommy's head, the brown spruce needles had the smell of dog fur on them. He turned to smell the spruce in the needles but the branches, and then the leaves, came together above and started carrying on, jostling with each other. Tommy closed his eyes.

Voices—down at the harbour. Girl voices. The McAdam kids. They were always making a racket. Tommy stirred, got up and walked down through the woods to the shore.

Yes, that's just who it was, the McAdams—Margaret, Rosie, Janet, and Little Wendy. The whole pack. They were farther up the shore, and the sound of them in the water and splashing each other was all along the shore. Tommy was down on the rocks, where he could see them, he was looking over and not moving. The girls were naked. All of them, except Little Wendy—she was on shore and laughing and too young anyway. Bare-naked! They were in the water; two of them were pushing out Auld Donny Boyd's boat.

Tommy ran up to the camp.

He went into the camp to get Wayne, Jimmy and Billie. They were sitting, smoking. Jimmy was out near the entrance, in the sun. He was at his arm with a knife, carving his initials into it. He looked up, keeping the knife tip where it was.

"What do you want, ya little prick?"

But that came from Billie, who was further inside the camp, back out of the sunlight. Billie had a moustache and was always at it, licking. Wayne was in beside him, out of sight.

Tommy could see Billie's arm in the shadows. There were thin strips of scabs on it where he had carved in, "B.M."

"Rosie McAdam and the girls are naked down at the shore!"

All rose.

"Let's go, boys, dippers—and if you're lyin', ya little prick, you're gettin' your teeth to drink!" Wayne got up.

There was a lot of happiness. The four boys, Tommy trailing, tore off down through the spruces and down over the slopes to the shore. But they quieted and slowed when they came to where the trees ended and the roots in the banks of the shore began. The smell of moon-tide seaweed was in the harbour air. The others did the same as Wayne, the eldest. He was down on his belly and was crawling neatly over the big shore rocks—the ones with pockets of water in their top cracks. There had been a big tide and the water had come up over them. Only yesterday Tommy had been down here and had been putting snails and starfish into the pockets of water. The starfish were still there.

The girls were still there.

They were on shore now and stepping into their pants.

"Me son, look at the fly bites on that Margaret," said Jimmy who, like the others, had turned still and was pressed down behind some higher rocks.

"Shut up," Wayne said, his eyes and body narrow like a soldier's.

The girls had their shirts on now and the shirts got pasted on their fronts and backs as they had no towels. They were on their way home now and it got a little sad but Wayne, brave and decisive, knowing the end of the spectacle was at hand, rose to his feet, to his full height. He flung his arms out and started screeching. This was the signal for Jimmy and Billie. Even Tommy was up and enjoying himself, flailing at the air and hollering. The McAdam girls froze where they were on the rocks of the bank. They moved then and screamed their high pitches. The whole shore filled with screaming.

Margaret and Janet, the older ones, changed their screams to curses, commands and threats. They bent for rocks to throw. Rosie took Little Wendy up into the woods—she had to take care of her as Little Wendy was her baby sister and too young to be down at the shore. The rock throwing started then but the boys were superb and dangerous. So twisting away from the rock throwing, Margaret and Rosie retreated, going up to where the first two younger girls were waiting above on the bank and in the trees. Their group of four then headed up the slopes below the trees, their rocks not even having come near the boys.

"C'mon," Wayne announced. "A boat."

The boys moved over the rocks with only the sound of their scuffs against the rocks now that the harbour was empty of all hollering.

They moved faster and skipped over to where the McAdam girls had left the boat. The girls had not tied it to shore in all the confusion of the attack and it was drifting. There was an old ice-clamper pole up on the bank. The boys used this to reach the boat and guide the boat in. Slow, slowly and heavily, the boat came into the rocks. It was a dinghy, an old one but sitting high in the water.

"Any oars for her?" Billie said, seeing there were none.

"I know where they are," Tommy said. "They're hid up in the woods, below the swinging tree."

"Well, fly the hell up and get them! Hurray it up too, b'y," Billie said.

Tommy returned with oars. They were handmade and heavy, old and solid. They had been painted white but the paint was nearly gone off them. It had not been boat paint. Black initials were on the handles of them.

Wayne took the oars and fit them in the tole pins that were already there and sticking up out of the sides of the boat. The others got in and the boat rocked with their weight.

"Why don't we leave him on shore," Billie said of Tommy, who was at the front, kneeling on a coiled length of fishing rope.

The boat went through the water with Wayne rowing. He was putting his back into it but was not a good rower. He was the eldest. Tommy looked down at the fish-coloured water they were going through, the bottom below going further and further down until it went completely out of sight where the colour of the water richened to black. They were heading for the other side of the harbour, toward a fog bank, toward lobster traps.

When they were halfway across, Billie took over at the oars and they started going around in a circle. He was putting too much of the right oar into it. Jimmy tried. He was better. But the boat began to struggle out in the middle where the wind was up high and solid.

No one had been out here before, not at this time of year.

In winter they might have, when there was plenty of ice. It was a new place to view things now. They could even see the houses of Niganiche. The houses were high above the harbour. They looked quiet, strange and peaceful from here, sitting perfectly where they were and belonging to no fixed pattern, looking as if some giant thumb and some giant finger had set them up where the ground was most stable.

A fog bank, like the one the boys in the boat were headed for, was up in the mountains just above the community. It was lowering

Carving Initials

itself down onto the community and might soon be hiding it. This would help.

Sitting up there in one of the houses was Auld Donny Boyd, the owner of the boat. He had his binoculars in his hands and was doing what he always did: he was looking down at the harbour. He saw the boys in the boat. He knew each boy's family.

He put his binoculars on the table, stood up and got out the phone book. It was on the chair beside the fridge, above his rubber boots. He carried the phone book to the table, laid it out. He picked up his binoculars again. They were halfway across now, the thieving little bastards. They were heading for in under the fog bank that was there on the other side, close to the Point, right near where the McAdams first lived in Niganiche, the best place in the whole harbour for lobsters. Nice bottom there. Auld Donny Boyd used to set his own traps there—so had his father—in that very same spot, right over there. Those traps were always a treat to pull, too, after a day of being out below Smokey Mountain, where it was open water and sometimes rough as hell. It was always nice to reach the harbour when you were finished out there. The last Auld Donny Boyd heard, the fine for pulling lobster traps was two thousand dollars. There might even be a prison term in it now. It was no simple crime, messing around with a man's living. Those young bastards won't even get a slap on the wrists, though. Still—a good scare from the Fisheries officer, that might fix them.

"Jimmy, me son, I can see your house from here!" Billie said.

"Look," Jimmy said. "Up over there a bit, Auld Donny Boyd's house, the old bastard with the head bald enough to write a song about."

"Bald? Fuck bald—we're just lucky he's blind! If he wasn't we'd all be off to prison in Dorchester by now. It's his boat, ya know, so hurry it the frig up and get us buried in the fog bank."

Billie was going through a tackle box he found under the back seat; he was throwing rusted lures and smelt hooks out into the water. Some line attached to one of the hooks, a big trout hook, and when Jimmy adjusted his weight his foot came down hard on the stray line. The line tightened and shot the attached hook forward, digging it soundly in through Billie's baby finger, in under the nail. Billie let out a screech that went out into the fog bank, and the echo of it went straight up into the mountains above the harbour.

"You stupid, stupid bastard! You stupid bastard…."

Jimmy was paused in his rowing. Billie was holding his finger and the big spray of the fishing twine was curved above the finger. There was no blood, but the finger was fattened where the hook went in. Jimmy was waiting to start up the rowing.

Wayne spoke: "Don't be such a souk, b'y."

Wayne laughed.

Jimmy laughed too and when Tommy opened his mouth to laugh he could see tears forming and thickening the colour in Billie's eyes. And the eyes were looking firmly at Tommy and no one else.

"I'm gonna kill you when we get ashore," Billie said. "I swear to fuck almighty, you're dead."

But Tommy, being at the front of the boat, disappeared first into the fog, which then eased itself over every other boy and over the whole boat.

The screen door of Auld Donny Boyd's house yanked, shook and opened.

It was Rosie. Auld Donny Boyd could see Little Wendy out through the glass in the door. She was standing on the step, hands behind her back, small and beautiful and still as only a child could be. Something had happened.

"Grandfather," Rosie said. "Wayne MacQuarrie and them stoled your boat and took off in it! I seen them goin', they're out in the harbour rate now!"

Auld Donny Boyd told Rosie to go out and play, to look after Little Wendy.

A heavy mist was in Auld Donny Boyd's yard now. It was darkening all the colours, especially the green of the grass. One of the girls bent down and set up lines for hopscotch in the clay of the driveway. Auld Donny Boyd went back into the kitchen and took off his eyeglasses. When he had heard someone at the door, he had put them on. He placed them on the table.

Young Rosie had given him a good fright—but anyone would, for that matter, coming into the house like that, not calling first. At the table he fit the eyeglasses back into their special case.

Auld Donny Boyd had the telephone number for Fisheries out in front of him. He looked at it. The numbers were not hard to make out at all. But it would be a lot better if they were hard to make out, wouldn't it?

It was a good fourteen years now since Auld Donny Boyd had come in off the water. At first, when it happened, when his eyes had started to go after spending the better part of his life out there, he was all upset. He cursed his body for having gone to hell while he was still fairly young and still able to do a good day's work. It was the swordfishing. That's what did it. Staring out from a boat at the sea calms, the sea flats—day in day out, searching for a fin that was never any wider than a hair. What a life for a man to be involved in—silver and tin, sea colours, that was all that ever came back to your eyes. Looking at the sun for a living, is what it was. Nothing more. A couple years of that will tear the eyes out of anyone, don't matter who you are.

And then he had to go through the whole racket of proving to the compensation people that his eyes really were bad. And them, those people—doing everything they could to tell him he could go back out, insisting he could keep fishing, or get some work elsewhere. But what else, what other work in the name of God was there? For him? He listened to them, though, went back out and started up again. That is, till the day he went out and couldn't get back in. That fixed them! They weren't skeptical after that.

Then when the cheques started arriving in the mail—the first going off, anyway—Auld Donny Boyd didn't think it right for anyone to sit around and get money for it. No. But what could he do! There was no work, not even a stick of wood to be carried in the woods for anyone! No jobs—all this happened in the fall of the year, anyhow. Then, before long, a few months into that lifestyle and there was no other. He got comfortable—anyone would—he got comfortable with the situation. Sitting around, the cheques. It became all there was.

Then, when his eyesight started coming back to him, he was angered at first. They had just been strained was all, the eyes; it had been awfully dry that summer, there had been no wind when they went. And it was only natural that he did what he did next, any man would do the same—the making out, the pretending that his eyes were still bad, still gone, still shot. It became second nature, like everything else. It became just something additional to the sitting around and the waiting for the cheques. A man was trapped one way or another, anyway, sooner or later he's trapped.

Auld Donny Boyd looked down at the number of Fisheries in the book. It was one of those numbers that was easy to remember. It had the lower digits in it and there was repetition. But there would be an official report if he called. They would ask him how he knew the boys were out there, down in the harbour. His granddaughter Rosie had told him, he could easily say that—because she had after all. But no, no he wouldn't chance it; he didn't trust them Fishery bastards. Never had.

There was a break, a window in the fog. Tommy still at the front of the boat could see the road on the other side of the harbour. There was a straight stretch there. A white car was driving down. Someone else was out on the road, too, on a bike. A woman, older. It was one of the Boones, Jessie Boone. Tommy knew that she was somehow related to Billie, who never liked her mentioned. She was his mother, was one report. She lived alone over there, on the other side of the harbour. What went around in the community was that she was drunk every day of the year 1974. She never went to church. Did she ever look strange on the bike, her being old and alcoholic!

She came farther up the straight stretch and Tommy could

hear her come. When she was closer he could see that the bike she was on was his own. The break, the window in the fog, closed and Tommy saw nothing again. The boat brushed up against a lobster trap buoy, it was red and green, and from the markings on it, the boys could see that it was one of Jew McAdam's.

Jimmy pulled the oars in to himself, and the boat went on its own as if suddenly underneath was a sheet of ice. Wayne was fast. He had his hand out in the water, underneath and taking a hold of the rope that went down at a deep slant under the buoy. He yanked the rope up free of the water and started hauling it in. The boat got more stable with the steady and solid pulling up of the lobster trap from below. Tommy looked at Billie, who had the finger now wrapped in a piece of striped cloth. The cloth came off the lower part of his shirt. Wayne had used his pocket knife to cut the piece off for him; Billie had done up his finger in it himself. It was a tiny stained turban now. Billie saw that Tommy was looking:

"And don't think you're still not getting your death—'cause ya are."

Tommy turned away. Billie went on to say that as soon as they were out of the boat Tommy was getting a puck in the teeth. Billie finished and turned down at the water where the trap was being pulled. Tommy stole a glance and saw that the hook was in the finger of the right hand. What was he going to hit him with? Tommy looked up at Billie's face. He would mention the bike if he had to. Even though it didn't feel like it anymore, it was his after all.

As the trap came closer to the surface the boat began to tilt more.

"Youse fellas get your weight over to the other side," Wayne said.

Tommy watched Billie. He was moving away from the hauling of the trap. Tommy could not move to help offset the weight because it was narrow where he was. He looked instead at the ugly tight knot in the flesh of Billie's young forehead. Tommy felt sorry for him. Billie really was ugly and would stay this way. Here in the boat, with the hook in his finger, brought all this out.

Then the trap broke clear of the water with a sucking and gushing sound. It nearly upset the boat when Wayne, with Jimmy's help, hoisted it inside. Billie and Tommy sat upright where they were, like two altar boys, looking quietly at the trap. Wayne turned the two slimy wooden latches and then tugged at the door to the trap. There were lots of crabs inside, backing themselves up against the sides of the trap; there were sea urchins, too. Tommy saw the lobsters right away. They were noble and ready, not hiding like the crabs, not useless like the sea urchins. Hiding was pointless.

Jimmy and Billie let out squeals as if they had never seen lobsters before. But it is true that these lobsters were different. They were purplish-black in colour.

It's just like when me eyes were bad, thought Auld Donny Boyd. He was full of agitation now that he could no longer see the boat in the fog bank on the other side of the harbour. But he kept his binoculars on the fog just the same: he saw the little bastards go in and had a good idea where they would come out.

The fog stayed like a batch of cold boiling milk. Those were Jew McAdam's traps over there and Auld Donny Boyd had thought of calling him directly. But Auld Donny Boyd had had an awful falling out with Jew's elder brother when they were not much older than those boys down there in the harbour. It was over something stupid—and when wasn't it? Auld Donny Boyd didn't want to think of it. "Gold's blue," Jew's brother had said. Auld Donny Boyd had piped up, called him a fool, saying it was not blue. They were boys, but they argued over it as anyone else would, and they wouldn't leave it go either, that is, until Jew's elder sister came over. "You're both fools," she said. "Gold? It's red!"

Yes, they were kids then and fought like kids, but that didn't stop the sister from taking a good-sized cut on her lip where one of the boys had struck her. To this day the mark of it was still visible, especially in church, especially when she was on her way back from communion. So telephoning Jew McAdam now, well, that would sure as hell be the right thing to do but it would mean a day or two of both parties thinking over what had been done to the man's sister's lip. And what was the point in having to deal with that on top of everything else?

The sister never married.

However, there was another way, as Auld Donny Boyd had never been without ideas when the situation called for them. Yes, he had almost worked himself up enough to do it too, to call into Fisheries—but to do it by not being himself. Yes, he might pull it off—he would make out like it was old Pip Donaldson doing the telephoning. She had more eyes than a potato patch, more ears than a whole field of ripe corn. She knew the dirt on people before it even happened, that one. Yes, making out like it was old Pip. And the best thing was that he would enjoy himself doing it.

"Hello," he said to himself. "Hello," he said to himself again raising the binoculars. "There are some boys pulling traps in the harbour, hello?" He said the hello one more time and then stood laughing, shaking the binoculars on the bridge of his nose. That old gossipy twang in her voice, it was nothing to get down. The old thing is right here in the kitchen herself, he laughed.

And Auld Donny Boyd owed Pip Donaldson, anyhow. She was the one who had gone on to everyone at the card game that his eyes were not at all bad, that he was making most of it up. She talked about it at bingo, too. She was who was spreading around that he was faking it so that he could come in off the water and collect a nice little government cheque. Ooh, that miserable old troublemaker! The old tool-of-misery!

But the real thing was that it was she who had come between Auld Donny Boyd and a young one from North Niganiche many years back. I don't even want to think of it, he said to himself, out loud now. Pip Donaldson was rotten, had been all her life. The old rig had something coming to her. Trouble was, she was so slimy, so crafty. She would find out who made the call. Her? Easily. And that would be something else she could use against him, the situation with his eyes.

Auld Donny Boyd did not feel like calling anyone anymore,

anyhow. He raised his shoulders. He laid the binoculars down on the table and shut the phone book. And right down there in my boat, he thought! Right down there, it was her own grand-nephews that were now down there in my boat! Them thieving young MacQuarrie bastards. Plain as day it was them all right, which made it her sister's grandchildren.

There was a gun rack above the radio. Auld Donny Boyd reached up and took down the rifle. A crack of air was under the window and Auld Donny Boyd poked the barrel of the rifle through, careful around the sill with the tip of the barrel, careful with the gun's sights. But the wood of the lower part of the window was in the way of the gun scope. A book was under the window holding it up. The Bible. It was lying flat on its side. Auld Donny Boyd brought the whole gun back in, raised the window and set the book upright under it. The air that was across the yard moved into the kitchen and a good bit of frost that was in it yet came with it. The barrel was back out the window again. Auld Donny Boyd could see perfectly now. The scope was much better. Yes, it was ten times what the binoculars were, and only one eye was needed to use it. He scanned the fog bank. Yes, the scope, that was the thing to use here to see them with but that was not why he had taken the gun down. The air from outside moved in and down his chest.

Half a dozen fair-size lobsters were now snapping slowly at each other in the back of the boat. Most were hidden under the seat. Tommy could tell that Billie was scared to death of them and with the hook driven in his finger at the same time, it was a rough time for him. A sea gull moved above, delivering a thin and quick shadow over the length of the boat, flying in a small patch of the sun that was now busy stripping apart fog in around the lobster traps.

"There," Jimmy said at last, balancing the final trap on the side of the boat. "That's the last of them. C'mon, the sun's coming out," he said, looking at Wayne. "Let's go," Billie said, hopefully now, looking toward shore on their side of the harbour. Tommy heard the gentle splash of the last lobster trap as it hit the water. As the

Carving Initials

others had done, it sat on the surface a moment, the harbour water filling in over the top of it and making its lathes ripple. The ripples were waves of good-bye, the thing went unwillingly back down into the black of the harbour.

Wayne was at the oars now and was hauling hard on the left oar only to swing the boat around to point its bow back for the other side. His first even draw at both oars hardly moved the boat at all but after putting his back into the second and third draw, the boat found its speed.

Above, the fog was being shredded and sliced. Pieces of it hung in wisps and the heat from the sun began to burn and feel good over the jeans of the boys.

Then, there were three sharp snaps in the wood of the boat. They came like rocks snipping off the necks of floating beer bottles. Jimmy went down to his foot. Next came the three claps of thunder from up high in the mountains above the harbour and all through the houses of Niganiche. And after reaching the boys in the boat the echoes proceeded across the harbour and well up over the ski hill mountain. A flock of ducks, frightened by it, were flapping and beating apart the air above the clam flats, where they had been feeding. They were heading out of the harbour.

Jimmy was undoing the lacing of a sneaker and saying plainly that his foot was stinging and boiling hot. He rolled down his work sock, the others saw the thick purple hole that was just under the ankle. The foot looked like a rotten plum was in it. Jimmy started crying. Billie stared. Tommy, from the bow, told Jimmy to get some sea water on it, to take his shirt off and wrap it. Wayne rowed. Tears fell in the boat. The lobsters were no longer snapping at each other and with the sun on them now, they would not make shore.

David Muise

Paste Wax

I LOVE THE SMELL OF PASTE WAX in the morning.

I am in a small bakery in rural France where I join the long line of early risers anxious to buy fresh bread for breakfast. The shop is spotlessly clean with a brightly coloured tile floor which, to my delight, emits the sweet aroma of freshly applied wax.

The slightest whiff of paste wax takes me back to my childhood home where it is always Saturday morning and my mother is on her knees applying a coat of Johnson's Paste Wax to the floors. My brothers and I sit patiently, our father's thick wool socks on our feet, anxiously awaiting her signal.

Task completed, she rises up to her full five feet and says, "Go to it boys…and try not to kill each other"—and all manner of mayhem breaks loose. We are world class skiers swooshing down the Alps, Yogi Berra sliding into second base. We run. We slide. We fall over each other in joyous laughter as the Montreal Canadiens crash the net wreaking havoc on the hapless, and hated, Toronto Maple Leafs.

Sadly, our joy will be taken away some years later when my father, ever the romantic, gives Mom an electric floor polisher for Christmas.

I always wanted to travel but poverty and responsibility kept me grounded. In school I loved Geography and bristled when I received a mark less than one hundred percent. When asked what I wanted to do when I grew up, "See the whole world" was always my answer.

A number of friends bummed around Europe after high school, *Europe on $5 a Day* protruding from their maple-leaf-festooned backpacks. Not me. I was working five night shifts a week at the Sydney Steel plant, saving for university.

At university we passed many an evening reliving tales of student parties in Paris, summer romances in Rome and just the whole goddamn wonder of it all. I was living vicariously through my better-heeled friends, reading travel brochures (no Internet in those days) and watching every travel program that our two television channels carried. Post cards they had sent me were proudly displayed on my bulletin board in hopes that I might soon return the favour. Following graduation another group departed for Europe, some members for the second time, while I donned my steel-toed boots and headed back to the steel plant, law school tuition to be earned.

Now, at the age of 61, I am finally in Europe. I have the obligatory maple leaf flag on my backpack but *Europe on $5 a Day* is forgotten as well as impossible. I am traveling alone. I have time to think and reflect.

My reverie is broken as what I assume is an apprentice baker heaves an armload of baguettes, fresh from the oven, onto the counter. The aroma is intoxicating. I am reminded of a magazine article I read that chronicled a series of scientific studies which hailed the sense of smell as the one most likely to evoke long-buried memories. A smell can bring on a flood of memories because of a little part of the brain known as the olfactory bulb which forms a vital part of the limbic system, an area associated with memory and feelings.

That's why whenever I encounter the now rare but still acrid smell of coal smoke, I am reminded that my home, Cape Breton, was once coal mining country. King Coal heated and lighted our homes; its ashes rendered our sidewalks safe and freed many a stranded car from an icy ditch. To us kids the ubiquitous clinker was our hockey puck, great lumps of No. 26 coal our goal posts. Shinny under a street lamp on a cold winter's evening was as glorious as a Saturday night contest at Montreal Forum. We were Rocket Richard and Jean Beliveau as we flew down the icy street on gum-booted feet, scoring magical goals to the delight of an audience of stray cats and mean-looking dogs. Our flights of fancy brought to an abrupt end not by the sound of the Forum's siren but by the ringing of the Angelus from the nearby church at six o'clock, a signal that supper was ready and you had better get to it.

Expose me to the sweet and sour combination of Old Spice and cigarette smoke and I am fourteen again and my father is teaching me the art of shaving. Balancing his Export Plain on the edge of the sink, he swirls a brush in a soapy cup like he was whipping fresh cream. He then slathers my face with the foamy concoction, adjusts the Gillette Super Blue blade in his ancient safety razor and hands it to me.

"Try not to cut your throat, you hairy little bugger, your mother just waxed the floor."

I am shaving because I am off to my first high school dance. A shy and awkward teenager in my older brother's ill-fitting suit and my dead grandfather's shoes, I break into a cold sweat at the thought of asking a girl to dance. My heart broken by rejection I stand in the corner with my friends, kicking at the Dustbane-laced sawdust the janitor is sure will protect his precious parquet floor from pounding feet. Years later I will read on the Dustbane website all of their products are now environmentally friendly. My memories do not confirm this boast, at least not in my teenage environment.

Now I am lying on a hard hospital table staring blankly at the ceiling, an ancient Cobalt machine buzzing above my stomach. I am twenty-one. Twenty-one-year-olds are not supposed to have cancer. I hear the hum of the the electric motor as it turns the machine to another spot on my body. I must go through this ritual twenty-nine more times before the doctors can assure me that all the bad cells have been destroyed. My university studies are on hold. My wife cries as she holds our newborn daughter next to my hospital bed. I hate the smell of ozone.

Back in the small French bakery, the aroma from the steamy baguettes sends me into a Pavlovian frenzy. Once more I see my mother. She is swatting me with a dishtowel as I try to extricate the heel, arguably the best part of the loaf, from the bread she has set out on the cupboard to cool. As I open my eyes I half expect to see her coming around the end of the counter, dishtowel at the ready. But I am safe, she has never been to France. She is thousands of miles away, back in Cape Breton, probably waxing her kitchen floor.

"Monsieur?"

"Monsieur? Qu'est-ce que tu désire?"

I smile. What do I wish? Nothing, really. The simple smell of paste wax and freshly baked bread have taken me on a trip that none of my friends—regardless of their means—could ever imagine, let alone share. I tuck a baguette into my backpack, tip my toque to the baker and head out into the early morning street in search of a phone booth so I can call my mother.

Sue McKay Miller

Driving to Dolores

WE WERE CRUISING THE PRAIRIE BACK ROADS, high on homegrown and grooving to a Dead bootleg from the '70s. Well, maybe to say we were cruising is a slight exaggeration. A rare rain had turned the clay into a sticky sludge that sucked at our tires and tried to lure the big Suburban into one ditch or the other. The moon was bathing the barren land in spooky silver light and we were all a bit delirious with moonshine and beer.

I took a draw on my brew. We had a couple of buckets full. Literally. We'd taken them with us, buckets and all, when we staggered out of the Farengo Hotel in the wee hours. The tavern in Farengo was the preferred drinking hole for bikers and cowboys and misfits like ourselves. It was the only place where I'd ever ordered a bucket of beer and got a bucket full of bottles of beer and nothing else. No ice. The opened beers just sat there in the bucket on the table, getting warmer and flatter. Or they would have, except that there were six of us and the beer buckets emptied fast and furious. Now we six were in the Suburban, or the Burb as Jo called it, three pairs of bums on three rows of seats, creeping the ten or fifteen miles back to the town of Dolores. Dolores. Three syllables, as in Duh-LOR-us. Rhymes with that hidden forbidden sweet-meat treat.

"Jesus, Jo. Pick it up a little. We're never gonna get there." That was Jo's old man, Karl.

"Honey, this mud is slippery as spring slush. And I want to make sure we get there in one piece." Jo's feathers were hard to ruffle. Good thing, since Karl tended toward irritable at the best of times and could be downright morose when he was pickled.

I wanted to give him a little thump on the head but there was a row of seats between Jo and Karl and me. Al and Mona had come up from Moose Jaw and sat in the middle row. I sat in the back next to my buddy Tucker. It was down to him that I was here in the first place. Down to him and a drunken wager.

It had all seemed like good fun at the time, sitting in the university staff lounge and working on our second martinis. Or was it our third? The three-martini lunch had died of cirrhosis sometime in the '60s, but Tucker and I like to resurrect it once in a while, playing hooky and whiling away the afternoon in a haze of gin-induced philosophy.

"What are you up to this weekend?" he'd asked, popping an olive beneath the bristles of his rusty moustache.

"Heading for the hills, my friend." The foothills, that is. My favourite wilderness getaway, where ancient tectonic forces had ploughed the Rockies into the prairie's sediments until the rock buckled and warped like a bunched-up rug.

"I'm meeting a few friends in Dolores this weekend," he said. "Why not check it out?" Dolores. I had heard about the prairie ghost town before, on some other martini-soaked afternoon.

"No thanks, my friend. You know what they say—go west, young woman."

"That was back when the west was wild. Now everybody and his dog goes west every weekend. Be different. Head east. That's where the real adventure is."

"Adventure? In the prairies? Tucker, there's nothing out there."

"Wanna bet?"

"It's dead flat and deadly boring."

"Wanna bet?"

"The prairies are basically the porridge of landscapes. No snap, no crackle, no pop."

"Wanna bet?"

"Tucker, you have a scratch on your CD."

"So answer my question."

Question?

"Do-you-want-to-bet?"

"Bet what?"

"Bet that I'm right and you're wrong. Come to Dolores this weekend. Then if you still think the prairies are boring, you win."

"Wonderful. And for sacrificing my weekend, what do I win?"

"My ammonite."

I had to keep myself from drooling into my martini. I'd never coveted Tucker's ass, but when it came to the fantastic fossil he kept in his office, I'd broken the Tenth Commandment more than once. It was the biggest ammonite I'd ever seen.

"And if I lose?"

Tucker pointed at the tooth dangling around my neck. I reached up and clutched the fang on its leather thong. It was smooth and curved, the colour of aged ivory. An old woman selling jewellery at a folk festival had watched as I picked it up and rubbed it between my thumb and fingers. "Coyote tooth," she'd said. "The shape-shifter. It's meant for you. Coyote is your totem." She probably said that to everyone who showed any interest in the necklace, but I'd taken it to heart. And that's where the tooth had hung ever since, just above my heart. My talisman.

Now a wise person would not make a wager under the influence of martinis. But then a person under the influence of martinis is seldom wise. I'd had plenty of time for remorse during the three-hour drive to Dolores, which had stretched closer to four because I kept getting lost on the back roads. I'd figured driving through the prairies was so dead simple that the only danger was in nodding off from sheer boredom. Maybe that was because I'd never strayed off the highways into the elaborate maze of gravel back roads. I'd also assumed that the prairies were as dry as parched bison bones, but my pickup slewed and slithered like a stewed sidewinder on the greasy roads.

I'd cursed Tucker and his wager even as I recalled his warning. "Keep checking your rearview mirror. If you see a little black cloud, keep an eye on it. If that black cloud starts filling your mirror, it's gaining on you. Prairie storms like to sneak up on you from behind. Hunt you down and chew you up and spit you out."

Driving in the night before I hadn't seen anything but blackness in my rearview mirror. But the road churning beneath my wheels certainly seemed like it had been chewed up and spat out, which was why I was cool with Jo's sedate pace.

"Slow and steady, Jo, that's the way to go," I called out. At this speed, we could slide into the beckoning ditch or bump into a buffalo and not get hurt. I wasn't counting on Jo's reflexes to save us. She had a fairly novel interpretation of the duties of a designated driver. After downing her share of Lethbridge Pilsner beer she declared to the waitress in a loud voice, "No more for me—I'm the designated driver. Just tokes for me from midnight on." The other four patrons, bikers who were pals with the waitress, didn't bat an eye.

The three-piece country band kept belting out Hank Williams and Patsy Cline numbers and the hotel owner grinned at us from under the brim of a ten-gallon Stetson that matched his fringed buckskin chaps and snakeskin boots for cowboy caricature. We might have been in a spaghetti western directed by Federico Fellini.

My seatmate Tucker nudged me with his elbow.

"Hey," he said, nodding towards his window. "Look!"

I leaned over and peered out the window. There was a big white owl, moonlit wings flapping as he kept pace with us.

"What?" asked Jo, turning the steering wheel as she turned her head.

"Watch out!" yelled Karl and made a grab for the wheel. The suburban swerved a bit and started to skid but our tortoise-pace saved us from losing the road. I hardly noticed; I was too awestruck by that silver-winged flyer hugging our flank.

"A night spirit," I said.

I could see Tucker's teeth gleam in the moonlight as he grinned.

"It's a ghost! A ghost from Dolores out for a cruise."

Dolores. Our destination. Tucker had chanced upon the ghost town while working the surrounding rigs as a mud-logger. Now he and a few friends spent time out there whenever they could, in abandoned houses with peeling wallpaper and patchy linoleum and views that stretched out to eternity. There was a Legion in Dolores, but the windows were boarded and the taps were dry, forcing thirsty folk like us to roam across the prairies to Farengo in search of beverages. And now, all beveraged up, we were heading back to that gathering place of ghosts, that sanctuary for spectres and spooks. Dolores was an old frontier town straight out of that Fellini spaghetti western all right, but the script must have been written by Stephen King.

"That owl following us is creepy," said Mona. "It's like some kind of bad omen."

"Yeah," replied Tucker, all nonchalant. "Everybody knows that owls are omens of death."

"Jesus, Tucker! Don't say that! You're freaking me out!" Mona said, teetering on the edge of hysteria.

"Can it, Tucker," Al said, putting his arm around his wife. Mona wasn't used to toking. We'd all egged her on and it turns out it was pretty powerful shit. Organic, grown in dirt instead of a chemical bath, and not started from genetically buzzed-out clones but right from seed—a jaunty strain dubbed Blue Haze. Germinated and then lovingly nurtured with bat guano, teased by light and judicious pruning into producing succulent oozing buds, a female plant horny and yearning for pollination, flaunting seductive resins, blissfully unaware there wasn't a male in spittin' distance. The resultant little buddies were packed with THC.

I knew, because I grew it myself. Toker beware. Even I'd been surprised at its virginal potency, and the rest of the crew, old timers in the world of weed, were all a bit stunned. But it was my homegrown and I wanted Mona to enjoy the trip. Besides, her bad vibe was messing up my own mellow. Paranoia is like yawning, it's contagious.

"White owls are good omens," I said, deciding right then that it was true. Maybe omens assume whatever power we give them, whether good or malevolent. I slipped my left hand inside my jean jacket. Just an old tooth? Or talisman for a totem?

"I think owls are messengers from the spirit world," Jo said.

"Exactly!" Tucker declared triumphantly. "And the message is—we're all about to die and go to the spirit world!"

"Not if we pull over and *I* drive," grumbled Karl.

"No one's going to die," Al said. And then as if the owl heard Al's calm pronouncement and knew the jig was up, he started to move ahead of us.

"Jesus," Karl groaned. "We're being passed by a goddamn owl!"

As for that owl, bird or ghost or spirit messenger, he passed us and then flew right in front of us, his powerful wings beating up and down, lit up now by our headlights. There was a collective sigh in the truck as if we'd all been holding our breath.

"He's soooo beautiful," Jo said.

"Can you believe it?" groused Karl. "Beaten by a bird."

"Whoa—look at that!" exclaimed Jo.

"What the hell?" barked Karl.

"Oh shit!" cried Mona.

"See? I told ya—we're all gonna die!" yelled Tucker.

"Oh shit!" Mona said again. "What's it doing?"

It was landing. The great white wings fluttered and it slowed and stretched out its talons and then it landed, smack dab in the middle of the road. Its body was facing away but it turned its head 180 degrees in that freaky *Exorcist* way and stared right at us. Or, I suppose, at a pair of monstrous blazing headlight eyes bearing down on it.

"Move!" Jo hollered.

"Don't brake," said Al. "Hit the damn thing if it won't move."

"Don't hit it!" I squeaked.

Jo hit the brakes.

"Jesus, Jo! What the fuck are you doing?" Karl roared.

The Suburban swung into a slow motion skid on the mud.

"Oh shit!" Mona said yet again.

"We're all gonna die!" Tucker screeched, but there was laughter in his voice, not fear.

There was time for all of this ranting and discourse because we were spinning very slowly. Time had expanded in some Einsteinian kind of way as the Suburban spun under the moon on a slick prairie road while a white owl stared us down. All the hollering and cursing stopped and we were suspended in silence as we floated around, pressing against each other like passengers in a slow-motion Tilt-a-Whirl at the edge of the universe. Then the Suburban slid to a stop, facing the opposite direction we'd been going but still miraculously on the road, all of us unhurt and in a mild state of shock, sitting in stunned silence.

The Suburban, also apparently in a mild state of shock, promptly stalled and the silence was complete. The Burb's lights fluttered and died. I looked out the back window, seeking the yellow eyes of that moonbird that had played chicken with a Suburban full of primates and won, but the prairie had transformed from ghostly grey to bituminous black and there was no sign of the white owl. All around us was a dark void, as though we'd skidded into a black hole that had sucked away light and sound and time.

The silence strung out like an elastic, attenuating until it snapped and voices erupted into a chorus of babbling and cussing and squabbling. I left them to it and pushed open the door and stumbled out into the night, scanning the sky for moonlit wings. There was nothing. That bird had flown. Truth is I couldn't see much of anything at all. The lights had gone out on the prairie. The moon that had been buffing up everything to a silvery sheen had vamoosed, and the deep dark had swallowed up not just the owl but the road and the fields and the low-rolling hills. As if the black hole that had swallowed the Suburban had gulped down everything else too—the owl and the moon and the sky and the very earth itself. Kind of freaky.

I felt a glob of existential dread welling up out of my guts and reached over to touch the hard metal casing of the Suburban. I needed to reassure myself that the material world still existed. My hand touched empty space. There was nothing there. The Suburban and its passengers had disappeared into the Abyss.

"Hey, what're you trying to do? Poke my eye out?"

It was Tucker. I'd been reaching through the open door and his face walked into my hand as he climbed out to join me on the road. I breathed again. Tucker offered me a smoke and in the brave little flame of his lighter I saw colour and solidity, the metallic red of the Suburban, Tucker's ruddy skin and gingery moustache, the slender white cylinder of a cigarette. We lit up and breathed smoke into the moist chill air and that glob of dread settled back into its hidey-hole as the solid world re-emerged from the Void.

Everyone else got out too, stretching and lighting cigarettes. I looked westward to where the moon had been just moments ago. Deep black. A little black cloud must have covered the face of our nightlight.

"Look up," Tucker said, nudging me. I did, and what a sight!

La Luna had been outshining all the other heavenly hosts, but with that Prima Donna tucked behind the curtains, the stars had a chance to shine, and shine they did, scattered all over that anthracite sky like shimmering flakes of mica. The sky was absolutely cluttered with 'em.

"There are more stars in the prairie, I swear," Jo said, tilting her head back. Tucker reached into the back seat and grabbed one of the buckets of beer we'd absconded with and passed the bottles around and we swigged the warmish, foamy Pil. It was delicious.

"Hey guys!" Jo said. "That owl *was* a messenger, sent to make us stop and look at the stars."

"I've seen them before," Al said.

"It was just a goddam owl," Karl opined.

"I'm just glad we weren't all *killed*," Mona said, waving her cigarette at Tucker so that it traced a series of red arcs through the air. Very trippy.

The ground was too wet to sit on so we leaned against the flanks of the Suburban, heedless of the splatters of mud. Tucker climbed up onto the roof and stretched himself out spread-eagled under the infinite sky.

"Hey Jo, why don't you turn on the tape deck and crank up the tunes," I said. I wanted to listen to the climax of the "Dark Star" jam under that glittering cascade of pinpoints of light. Jo reached in and clicked the key while I scrambled up onto the rooftop and joined Tucker. Jo hopped onto the hood just below us and lit up a doobie.

I lay there under the creamy gleam of the meandering Milky Way while the eerie keening and whines of Jerry's guitar melded with the thrumming of Phil's bass and vibrated off into the darkness, hunting out the coulees and echoing off the stars. Bright stars, not dark stars. Dark moon, I thought after the tape ended, propping myself up on my elbows and looking around, but it was still gonzo.

"Okay folks, let's go," Karl said. "And this time *I'm* driving." No one argued. It was damp and cooling off, and we still had miles to go before we'd sleep. We piled back into the Suburban and Karl turned the key in the ignition.

Nothing. Nada. Rien.

He tried again. Zero. Zippo. Zilch.

And again. Diddly-squat.

This baby was bust. The battery had given up the ghost.

"Aw shit," said Karl. "Now what the fuck is this?"

"I don't like this," said Mona.

"You must've killed the battery, playing the tape deck," Karl said.

"Nah," said Jo. "Can't be. We weren't stopped long enough."

"What's going on?" I asked. Tucker and I were in the back again and it was hard to hear everything from the front. "Why won't it start?"

"I don't *know* why it won't start," Karl growled, trying again a couple of times.

"Don't flood it," advised Jo.

"I'm not gonna fuckin' flood it," said Karl.

"You have starting problems before?" asked Al.

"Only when it's forty fuckin' below," answered Karl.

"Maybe there's an alien spacecraft in the area," suggested Tucker. "The electromagnetic force field jammed the electronics."

"Thanks for your analysis, Scotty," said Karl.

"Beam me up."

But no one laughed. The downward drag of liquor had outgunned the high rise of pot and we were all tanking. It was dark and chilly and we were stranded, still miles from Dolores. Funny how a funky ghost town could start to seem normal, like a refuge from the yawning prairie night.

"Too bad we aren't at the top of the next hill," Jo said. "Then we could try a push start."

"Too bad your spirit messenger never thought of that," Karl said.

Tucker poked me with his elbow. I poked him back, but I got the point of his elbow. The prairies aren't actually flat. Another urban myth blown.

Karl got out and popped the hood. Jo handed Al a flashlight from the glove compartment and he joined Karl in some under-the-hood ruminations, shining the dull beam into the oily interior.

"I know!" Tucker piped up beside me.

Jo and Mona and I waited.

"We'll hitchhike into town!"

The weak joke underlined our predicament. There's the odd farmer living out there with all that land and sky, but farmers are a diurnal breed. Then there are the oil workers, migrating amongst the rigs that suck oil from ancient sea sediments the way roughnecks suck up beer in shady saloons.

But in the wee hours, there wasn't another soul out there—at least not one inside a living body. We weren't going to be rescued with a battery boost or a lift into Spooksville. Not even the cops prowled these lonely roads.

I shivered and stared into the black, feeling the jittery edge of Mona's anxiety. We were stranded—isolated and vulnerable and exposed. There were powers out there in that vastness, powers greater and more ancient than we wee humans. Forces of good and evil, forever circling each other as they wrestled and played through eons of—

"I gotta pee again," announced Jo, interrupting my metaphysical musings. Yeah, for all that musing, we are organisms that eat and excrete.

"Me too," said Tucker, following her outside.

Highly suggestible organisms.

"Me three," I said, yielding to groupthink.

I climbed outside. Karl and Al were still fumbling around under the hood. Mona shifted up to the driver's seat and turned the key each time one of the fellahs tweaked something and yelled "Try it now!" Still nothing. More muttering and fiddling and a flashlight that was almost out of juice. We were going to be stumbling through the mud in the dark if we didn't get the Burb going.

I couldn't see which way Tucker or Jo had gone so I walked back along the road a little ways. It seemed even darker than it had before. I looked up, seeking starry reassurance and one more hit of the cosmic high. But the stars had vanished. That weird cloud that had veiled la Lune had spread its voluminous black burka across the entire sky and it was dead dark.

I squatted by the ditch to empty my beery bladder. And almost tipped over backwards when the blackness was shattered by a dazzling sheet of white lightning. It flashed the world into being and I saw Tucker and Jo, caught in the spotlight, necking like a pair of hormone-laced teenagers. No wonder they were so quiet—their lips were sealed. Then the heavenly flashbulb strobed again and they sprang apart as if they'd been zapped by electric-lip shocks.

I scrambled to my feet, too distracted to care about the damp patch on my knickers. I was standing there posing as a human lightning rod when the air cracked as if an axe-wielding giant had split the sky wide open. And out of that crack roared a primal fury, bellowing across the prairie and setting everything atremble, including me. Lightning forked and flashed as rumbles like ancient buffalo herds thundered across the land.

Tucker's little black cloud. It had crept up while we cavorted and caught us with our pants down—literally in my case. Any moment now sheets of cold water would pour through that cracked sky. It was time to make like lightning and bolt.

I was zipping and buttoning when I caught an eerie glow at the crest of the hill behind the Burb. What on earth? Then the glow brightened and my beery blue-hazed brain lurched into gear.

"Car!" I yelled, but my words were swallowed by a grumble of thunder. Someone was coming after all—we were saved! But wait. Who—or what—would be out on this godforsaken road at this godforsaken time of night? Fear jolted through me. Oh no, please. Not that.

"Cops!" I yelped, and staggered towards the Burb. I needed to chuck those incriminating beer bottles into the ditch. And I couldn't remember where I'd stashed the Blue Haze.

Glow turned to glare and I glanced upward. And froze. There was a ball of fire on the crest of the hill. I stared as an enormous tumbleweed of lightning rolled down the hill, crackling and sparking. Ball lightning. Barrelling towards the back of the Burb, where Mona sat behind the wheel, blissfully unaware, and Al and Karl stood, the open hood masking the fiery destruction rolling towards them.

The sluggish circuit from eyeball-to-brain and brain-to-mouth connected and I began to holler at Al and Karl to WATCH OUT! I saw Karl turning towards me and I saw Al reaching into the innards of the engine and I saw that electrified orb bearing down and I screamed NO! and clenched with horror as the ball connected and there was a blinding blast of light and a spray of sparks and voices howling in the night.

Then a rumble and a roar as the Burb fired up, engine thundering, head and taillights flashing and horn honking like a gigantic goose. Al and Karl hooted and hollered while Mona revved the engine like a crazed motorcycle mama on her Hawg. Jo and Tucker came out of left field, Jo cheering while Tucker whooped and did a merry little dance. I just stood there, the proverbial deer frozen in those blazing headlights.

What the hell had just happened? I looked away from all the commotion and deep into the prairie night, but the lightning ball had vanished. Had it even been real? Or just some kind of electric crazyland hallucination?

"Okay, let's get outa here!" Karl yelled as he climbed behind the wheel. I broke out of my deer-trance and hightailed it to the Burb, climbing in beside Tucker. Karl hit the gas and did a slo-mo donut until we were facing forward again, then took off, skidding in the muck. The others chattered, giddy with relief, while I stared out the passenger window. In the distance, forks of lightning danced away beneath a swirling black cloak, chased by a thunderous herd of groans and rumbles. The last ragged veil of cloud whipped away, strewing crystals of light in its wake. The unclad moon bounced back onto centre stage, flashing pewter light off the humps and gullies carved out by glacial giants.

Then, in the moonlight, I caught a flash of movement. A silhouette, shifting between the silver and the shadow. Shape-shifter! I gasped and grasped the tooth dangling on my chest, twisting in my seat to watch that prairie prowler until he vanished back into the shadows.

"What's out there now?" Tucker asked, leaning in. "Another spirit messanger?"

I turned to him, wide-eyed and tongue-tied. His silhouette shifted against the silvery light outside, tufts of hair sticking out like a madman's.

"Now let me see," he said, resting his stubbly chin on his fist *à la* Rodin. "What was it you said about the prairies again? Aha! I remember. The porridge of landscapes. No snap. No crackle. No pop."

Coyote, legendary Trickster. I eased the leather thong up over my head and, without regret, placed the talisman around Tucker's neck. A wager lost, a world gained.

Julie Curwin

Killing Agnes Donakowski

IN MEDICAL SCHOOL, they start you right off with death. You're no sooner through the front door than they've assigned you a cadaver and instructed you to start cutting. Here is your first patient, they say, already dead. Some of my classmates found this a bit off-putting, this plunging straight up to the elbows—sometimes literally—into death, but I found it oddly comforting. Familiar. I'd been killing things for close to twenty years by the time I got to medical school.

Even now, I have only the fondest memories of those early days in the gross anatomy lab: long gleaming rows of stainless steel slabs, six students to a corpse; the sweet dizzying smell of formaldehyde infiltrating your pores and clinging to your clothing like napalm; the tight tanned cleavage of Lana Dupinsky bulging over the top of her lab coat as she bent across the table to make the first incision, from the sternal notch down to the xyphoid process of cadaver number fifteen, the instructor saying, "Press firmly so that you penetrate through to the bone," and me saying, "Oh yes Lana, yes, press firmly."

To myself.

I hope.

The best thing about the dead is this: You can't kill them. No matter how incompetent or unlucky you are. No matter how many voodoo hexes have been placed upon you by your seven-year-old straight-off-the-boat-from-Santiago-de-los-Caballeros cousin Francisca, in retaliation for mooning her prissy little group of friends at your own eighth birthday party. Not that I believe in all that voodoo rubbish—a master's degree in molecular genetics and twenty-odd years away from Hispaniola tends to cure you of that. Surely my propensity for turning living things into deceased things is nothing more than a statistical aberration. A life-long, ego-crushing, soul-destroying, nasty rotten bitch of a statistical aberration which just happened to begin immediately after Francisca performed her evil little rituals. But still.

Bubbles the goldfish was my first victim. Bubbles was one of those monstrous google-eyed freaks of genetic tampering. He swam lethargically in the Woolco pet department aquarium, his entire plump black body shimmying back and forth, mouth opening and closing as if the effort of dragging those ridiculous ornate tail fins along was just too much. The other fish, the non-mutants, glided past him with their sleek golden bodies, mocking him with their efficient angular fins.

If Bubbles were a kid, my eight-year-old brain reasoned, he would be a pudgy black kid with coke-bottle glasses. He would talk with a lisp and carry multiple asthma puffers. He would hate gym class. Bubbles was more than a fish. He was a soul-mate.

We bought him against the advice of the Woolco pet department fish lady. The outcome was predictable. When he died, I wanted to bury him in the back yard but Dad said the proper way to conduct a fish funeral was "burial at sea" by which he meant flushing poor Bubbles down the toilet while reciting a few words about what a good fish he'd been and how much he'd be missed. All with my older brother Pedro laughing hysterically in the background.

The next victim was Harriet the teddy-bear hamster, who was pregnant when my friend Jimmy Barnes gave her to me to babysit for the summer while Jimmy traveled around Europe with his parents. Harriet died, two weeks to the day after I brought her home, of the complications of childbirth—an infection of some sort, according to the vet—but not before we watched her give birth to five tiny pups, all cute and pink and blind and squirmy, and then promptly eat the heads off each one. Hamsters, the vet explained, do not deal well with stress.

You'd think I'd have sworn off rodents after that, but the guinea pigs, Jimi Hendrix and Janis Joplin, were next. I'm not sure what they died of, but it didn't take long. Then there was Jarred the kitten (killed by the neighbour's German shepherd) followed by Buffy the toy poodle (canine parvovirus) and after that we decided to stick to houseplants, which I also had a remarkable propensity for killing.

Medical school works like this: You spend two years learning from textbooks and dead people. Then, on the first day of your third year, you are handed a crisp white coat, a yellow name tag and a stethoscope, and released upon hospital wards full of sick people. I dreaded the first live patient who would test whether my deadly statistical aberration/curse-of-death applied to humans under my care.

Along with that little vixen Lana Dupinsky, I was assigned to ward 4-D, the geriatric medicine inpatient unit. An inauspicious start. Ward 4-D smelled of boiled eggs and doom, which smells like this: ammonia, talcum powder, overripe fruit, industrial disinfectant, infectious diarrhea, citrus deodorizer. I walked the length of the corridor feeling like an alien from a strange planet, searching for the conference room where I'd been told to report for orientation. Past the frail masses in their rubber-soled slippers and terrycloth robes; past the nursing station with its tidy rows of charts, its blinking monitors, its beeps and bells and harried voices; past Percival Smith who sat in a geri-chair near the nursing station and had his name PERCIVAL SMITH monogrammed onto everything he owned. I passed a neat row of wheelchairs containing hydroponic humans, IV pumps forcing fluid into rickety arms, catheter bags draining waste fluid out the other end. Vacant stares, clicking dentures, diapers, dementia, despair. It was no coincidence, it occurred to me, that the geriatrics ward was called 4-D.

We were given a brief orientation by the senior geriatrics resident, a tall, thin unshaven man with curly black hair and multiple motor tics, named Jeff Seminov. Jeff looked as if he hadn't slept in three days. He told me later that in fact it had been closer to four days, and that the double espressos made his tics worse. His shoulders shrugged and his eyes blinked and his head nodded jerkily. Not a man who inspired confidence. Jeff's "orientation" consisted of the following: we would meet him here in the conference room every morning at 8 a.m. for rounds. Outside of rounds, we were to figure things out for ourselves. We were not to page him unless someone was dying, and only then if they were dying of something interesting and/or unexpected. He finished his spiel with a dramatic head bob.

"Any questions, comments, deep dark secrets?"

"I kill things," I admitted.

"You *kill* things?"

"Well, not on purpose, but...."

He didn't wait for me to finish. "Okay then, Killer," he said, "you can take Mrs. Donakowski. Trust me, Killer, she's been in and out of this place more times than I can count and *nobody* can kill Agnes Donakowski." He handed me a piece of paper with her name and room number written on it and sent me to complete the admission process.

Agnes Donakowski's room was at the opposite end of the corridor. She was standing in the corner facing the wall when I arrived, a pale grey ghost in a flannel nightgown and pink slippers. She turned slowly toward me, twirling the sash on her robe like some geriatric striptease dancer. Her eyes were milky but fierce, the creases on her face impossibly deep, yawning canyons of sagging flesh as opposed to mere worry lines.

"You're black," she said.

"Well," I said, stupidly, "yes I am." Beads of sweat were forming on my forehead. "Miguel Vargas, senior medical student. I'm here to admit you."

I extended my hand. Was it customary to shake hands with patients when meeting them for the first time? I wasn't sure. And what was I to do if my first patient was a racist?

Oxygen hissed quietly through soft rubber tubing, which started in her nose and drooped down over her mouth like the whiskers of a cat. She didn't move. Crumbs of pink lipstick clung to the cracks of her dry lips. The tubing flapped up and down when she spoke.

"I had a black lover once," she said. "Ended badly."

Okay. I flashed her my most charming smile. "Well, Mrs. Donakowski," I said, "I'm sure that gentleman regrets the day he let you slip away. But we have some paperwork to get done."

It was Magic. If only my charm worked so well on Lana Dupinsky. Agnes grinned, her top dentures lurching forward and then clicking sharply back into place. Her eyes softened and—was it my imagination—or did I see a tear running down her cheek?

"His name was David," she said, so softly that I could barely hear her over the soft hum of the oxygen, "and it wasn't his fault. Times were different."

Agnes sat on the bed and extended her hand, finally, to shake mine. I didn't really know how to admit a patient but the forms were self-explanatory and Agnes was a forgiving audience. She answered "Yes dear" or "I'm not quite sure" to all of my questions.

"Did your family doctor tell you that you had congestive heart failure?" I asked.

"Yes dear."

"How long ago was that, Mrs. Donakowski?"

"I'm not quite sure."

"Have you been taking your Lasix?"

"Yes dear."

"What dose have you been taking?"

"I'm not quite sure."

"Do you live alone, Agnes?"

"Yes dear."

"Who is your next of kin?"

"I'm not quite sure."

And on it went. When I was finished taking her history, I examined her tiny shriveled body, the skin so pearly white and fragile-looking that I was almost afraid to touch her, afraid that my stethoscope would take the top layer right off. I noted the crackles at the bases of both lungs and the loud systolic heart murmur—or was that the sound of my own blood rushing through my ears? The tissue around her temples was drawn in and the hardened cords of her temporal arteries pulsed visibly beneath the skin. Her lips trembled and pouted rhythmically. Her breath smelled like sour milk.

I documented that she was a "poor historian" and read through the thick pile of charts that accompanied her. Mild dementia, the old records said. Severe left ventricular dysfunction. Three previous heart attacks. Bypass surgery. Malignant melanoma, successfully treated in 1975. Kidney failure. Liver failure. Chronic obstructive lung disease. Adult onset diabetes. Osteoarthritis. Osteoporosis. Major depression. Was there anything, I wondered, that this poor old soul had not endured?

"She has the Dwindles," the charge nurse said when I emerged from Agnes's room to write up my admission note, "and there's nothing you or I or anyone else can do about it."

I felt sick to my stomach. Percival Smith gave me a gummy grin and banged a set of car keys on his tray table.

That night I dreamed I was swimming in a giant aquarium with a strange bloated fish, its long fins drooping and dragging against the current. But the fish had Agnes Donakowski's face, the deep creases and the milky eyes and the pink lipstick, and the fish said to me, "You know, Miguel, you really should just flush me down the toilet. It's my time."

I saw Agnes Donakowski almost every day for the next three weeks. She dwindled. I fought back with every weapon in the arsenal of modern medicine. She dwindled some more. The more she dwindled, the more I fought back. Tubes and wires began sprouting out of Agnes' tired pruney little body—IV lines, naso-gastric tubes, chest tubes, urinary catheters, oxygen sensors, cardiac monitors. She looked like an oil refinery.

The diuretics we gave her for congestive heart failure had made her kidneys as dry as melba toast. They were shutting down in protest. When we backed off on the diuretics she developed pulmonary edema—she started drowning in her own fluids. She had bouts of delirium. She hallucinated, yelled for David, her lost lover, tried to climb over the bed rails, pulled out her IV lines and the nasal prongs that delivered her oxygen. And she screamed, over and over and over again, the same three words: I DON'T KNOW! I seemed to be the only one who could calm her down. When she was delirious, she thought I was David.

One night when I was on call, Agnes climbed out of bed at three o'clock in the morning and refused to go back. The grim beeper summoned me to the ward, where the nightshift staff sat huddled together in the nurses' station, as if they feared venturing out into the darkness alone. Percival Smith, who never seemed to sleep, sat next to them, quietly tapping two spoons together—a ninety-two-year-old infant, complete with diapers and toys.

Agnes stood beside her bed, staring at the floor. A tired bouquet of carnations wilted on her bedside table, a remnant of family obligations. There was no one left who loved Agnes Donakowski.

"Hello, Agnes," I said, keeping my voice low to avoid startling her.

She looked up slowly. Her lips were blue. "Is it true," she said, "that the Inuit put their old people out on an ice-floe and let them float away? You know, when they get sick?"

"I don't think so, Agnes."

"Because I wish they'd do that for me. Just put me out on the ice in the harbour and let me float away."

"It's August, Agnes."

"Shit."

"So maybe you should just go to bed and sleep on it for tonight."

"Okay."

It was almost too easy. I helped her into bed, making sure that she didn't get tangled in the IV lines and oxygen tubing. She clutched my hand and told me that I reminded her of her long lost love, David.

"He died in 1944," she said. "In Italy. Signed up just to piss me off. Idiot. "

"I'm sorry," I said, but Agnes was already asleep, snoring softly, still clutching my hand. I stood there for a moment just watching her. Her IV pump made soft clicking noises—soothing, sleep-inducing noises. My eyes were heavy. I felt like crawling in beside her. Down the corridor at the nursing station, I heard laughter. They were playing word games. Tonight's game: How many words could they come up with that meant "vagina"?

"Twat," one of them said, too loud. "Beaver."

"Bearded clam," I added, as I walked past them on the way back to my lumpy call-room bed.

Percival Smith gave a toothless giggle. I had read somewhere that after thirty-six hours without sleep, medical students score in the developmentally delayed range on IQ tests. I was guessing that this must be true because I was absurdly happy with myself, downright giddy, for this: I'd convinced an old, dying lady to go to bed and I'd come up with a clever, yet exceedingly vulgar, term for "vagina." It was going to be a long two years.

The next morning I found Agnes with her oxygen tubing wrapped around her neck. She was pulling it upward, trying to strangle herself. I took her hand and gently moved it to her side.

"You look like my friend David," she said.

"So I've heard."

Later the same day she was delirious again and screaming at the top of her water-logged lungs. I could hear her as soon as I stepped off the elevator. "I DON'T KNOW I DON'T KNOW I DON'T KNOW I DON'T KNOW...."

What was it, I wondered, that she didn't know? *Is there a God? Will the Toronto Maple Leafs ever win another Stanley Cup? What do I want for lunch?* All questions I had pondered myself that very day. And I didn't know either.

I walked into the room to find the geriatrics fellow, Dr. Seminov, and three nurses trying to quiet Agnes. She responded by increasing her volume: "I DON'T KNOW I DON'T KNOW I. DON'T. KNOW!!!" I admired her stamina, the sheer vicious purity of her existential angst. They were preparing to give her a needle full of anti-psychotic medication, to knock poor Agnes into a calmer oblivion. I moved behind the nurses, intent on staying in the background, but Agnes caught sight of me.

"Hello, David," she said, lowering her volume. "I just had the strangest dream."

The nurses moved aside and let me in closer to the bedside. Agnes gripped my hand with both of hers, wrapping her bony fingers around my palm.

"I dreamed I was still alive, David."

"You are still alive, Agnes."

"Goddammit."

"And I'm…." I started to say "and I'm not David" but caught myself and said, "I'm here now. It's okay, Sweetie, you get some sleep."

Within seconds she was snoring again, exhausted by her Olympic-caliber screaming bout.

Vera, the charge nurse, looked at me and nodded her head with something approaching respect. "She falls asleep as soon as you walk into the room. Every time."

"I have that effect on women."

In the end, this is how I killed Agnes Donakowski: As the result of her kidney failure, there was excess urea in Agnes's blood. The urea crystals made her itchy and she scratched herself until she bled. The drugs we gave her for the itching made her delirious again, floridly delirious this time—she didn't even recognize me as David—and we had to give her sedating medication to keep her from hurting herself. This caused her to develop urinary retention. The retained urine was a stagnant breeding ground for bacteria, which caused her to develop a urinary tract infection, which made her kidney failure worse and necessitated treatment with antibiotics. All of this made her even more delirious. The antibiotics killed off all the good bacteria in her gut and caused an overgrowth of the *clostridium difficile* bacterium, a nasty little microbe which in turn caused her to develop a grave condition known as toxic megacolon. Her abdominal x-ray became the case of the week at radiology rounds. The junior radiology resident told me that Agnes's monstrously distended colon was the most interesting abdominal film she'd seen since the guy who had swallowed an entire box of thumb tacks.

In my dreams, the Agnes-fish was swimming in tighter and tighter circles, chasing its own tail.

The last lucid thing that Agnes Donakowski said to me before she died was this: "You should ask her out. That girl whose breasts you're always staring at."

She passed away peacefully three days later, with me holding her hand. I wasn't sure what to write on the death certificate. Voodoo hex? A broken heart? Doctor-assisted Dwindles? Existential angst? Soul-crushing statistical aberration? I settled on "multi-organ failure" and left the document for Dr. Seminov to co-sign.

Three hours after Agnes Donakowski died, Jeff Seminov found me curled up like a fetus in the on-call room, about to give up on medicine.

"You're not serious," he said, "about this death curse thing?" His head bobbed and weaved. "Listen, Killer, you tried to save her and you were with her when she died. You learned a few things. Sometimes that's the best we can do. Her time was up."

He asked me if I would at least finish out the geriatrics rotation. I asked him if he would mind calling me something other than Killer.

Ellison Robertson

Anglers

WHEN HE'D FIRST BEEN LED THROUGH THE DOOR, he'd felt drawn to the old man's fishing gear hanging high on the back wall, but once he'd been told not to touch any of it, the compact leather, straw, and canvas cases became a focus of fascination during the hours he spent alone in the small cabin. There'd been no room for him in the crowded cottage. He was too big to join his mother and father and his sister and the baby in the one spare bed. It was his father who had suggested he might like to have the shed to himself. The boy readily agreed when his father used the word adventure, and he'd thought himself quite brave as his mother tucked him in that first night, though he was glad she thought to say he could leave the light on. To reassure himself, he'd said aloud, "I'm almost six. I'll be a big boy soon." She smiled and said, Yes, he was going to be quite the little man, which pleased him, but then she was gone, and as the shadows seemed to press nearer, he'd burrowed deep beneath the covers.

He liked it here now, he thought, away from the loud laughter and sharp-voiced arguments of the adults. He rolled over and stared again at the mysterious cases hanging from the hooks his grandfather—or maybe his friend Froggy Boutilier, who owned the cottages—had whittled from tree branches. As he stood within reach of them at the edge of the sagging, musty bed, he thought of how even the words the old man used for the gear yielded a curiously rich taste each time he rolled them across his tongue: Tackle, reels, creel, flies, rods, and, especially, lures.

He wanted desperately to touch them, to divine the ways in which these precise objects fit together, but the mere thought of reaching up for them called up the frightening image of the old man's scowling face, of the dry, down-turned slit of his mouth as he'd rumbled, "These are my things. Got that? You don't touch them."

They'd arrived at the cottage on Friday evening. It had been a day of surprises, but the boy felt an uneasiness creep over him as he realized they were going to stay the night. "Where will I sleep?" he repeatedly whispered to his mother. She just said, "Wait and see." They'd only lived in their new house for a few weeks and he wasn't even used to his room there, though he'd played there alone for hours each day, and stared from the window across the stretch of scraped bare ground separating the house from the coal mine, and beyond its black and rust red and silvery tin buildings and towers to the town with its low central hill on which stood a church, where he'd been several times, and a grey shingled school where he'd start in September.

They'd been driving on a narrow dirt road beside a lake when his mother had said with a tone of startled realization, "You're not going to the cottage?"

His father laughed and said, "I just need to see the old man."

"Does he know we're coming? Did you tell him?"

"How do you think I know he's up here? You know I wouldn't go to him for help if I could get it anywhere else. And I wouldn't go now if I wasn't sure things will work out soon so I can pay him back right away."

"If he'll give you a dime," his mother said softly.

His father punched her playfully on the arm like he did sometimes to the boy. "Don't always be so negative," he said like he was making a joke, but the smile slowly slid from his face.

"Who's the old man?" the boy asked, already half certain. His father ignored him, shifting gears and stepping on the gas as the car shuddered up a long rutted hill. His mother said, "Your grandfather."

"Papa's father?" he asked, though he knew he only had the one grandfather because Momma's father had died before he'd been born.

"Yes."

He'd seen his grandfather a few times since they'd moved to the town where he lived, where his father had been born, and he was curious to know more about him—even though he'd seemed unfriendly to the boy. He'd come to their house the day they'd moved in, had walked from room to room, with his polished shoes clicking loudly on the hollow-sounding painted wood floors. He'd paused to peer at a stain which ran down the living room wallpaper and traced a long, knobby finger across a crack in the hall plaster. And he didn't say one word. His parents had followed awkwardly behind him as if they wanted to keep an eye on him, and the boy had trailed after them, slowed by his responsibility of guiding his sister who was only a toddler. The old man hadn't said a word until he was standing in the open door and looking across at the mine. "You're going to live in a miner's house, I guess next thing you'll be working in the mine."

The boy pondered this advice. He thought maybe it was a good idea, his father was always talking about needing a job, but when his grandfather had left without saying anything else, his father had slammed the door and started yelling at them all to "get the lead out and put some goddamn order in this goddamn hole."

Twice after that he'd gone to his grandfather's house with his father. The house was interesting to the boy, though a little scary, a little like the old man because it was dark and silent, crowded with large, dark pieces of furniture on which there were lacy cloths and tiny figurines he longed to pick up but wouldn't dare, and numerous clocks that ticked loudly in the quiet rooms and bonged now and then. And the place was filled with the old man's smell—tobacco and strong soap and a sweetness like the dry, dead flower petals that lay here and there in small bowls decorated with tiny Chinese people.

His father and grandfather, both times, sat at the table in the kitchen. The first time they'd stared at him as if expecting something, and then his grandfather looked at his grandmother and tilted his head back at the boy. Her heavy body gave a startled heave as if she might topple over, but her feet shuffled forward and it was all right.

The boy knew she wasn't his father's mother, who'd also died a long time ago, but another woman his grandfather had married. He'd heard his father say she was like a ghost in that old house, though she seemed substantial enough to the boy, not at all like the floating transparent spirit he'd expected. She was nice to him once she'd pointed out the things that were too delicate to handle, and she'd set up a tiny table in the parlour, as she called it, where she placed a cookie and a glass of warm, faintly soured milk. "There now," she said, "you enjoy that and I'll make myself scarce." Then she'd slowly made her way upstairs, sighing at each step.

He'd pushed the milk aside and nibbled at the cookie, some instinct making him careful to catch the crumbs in his hand and carefully lick them up. At first there wasn't a sound from the kitchen but then he would hear a few quietly murmured words. Every so often a voice rose to a strained anger, then receded back to a strangled silence. He couldn't tell which one of them it was, they sounded so much the same.

The second time they went there, a week or so later, it was much the same, and the boy hoped they wouldn't go again. His father had been angry and impatient with him after they'd left his grandfather's, though he was like that anyway most evenings when he came home from hunting for a job. That's what he called it, "Hunting for a job," and the boy pictured him sometimes with the heavy rifle from the closet, the one he'd said was from the war, tracking a job that was somehow like a big animal he'd shoot and carry home all bloody. That was just his imagination though, which his mother said would take him far in this world. She didn't say where, just laughed when he asked.

Each day his father left in the morning, just as he had when he was working, and came home after supper. Sometimes he smelled of beer and he'd seem a little happier for a while, but then his mother looked sad and wouldn't talk to him all evening. Later he might hear her talking loudly to his father, as if she was saying all the words she'd saved up.

Then on Friday his father had come home in a car which looked new though he'd described it to the boy's mother as "Like new but a real steal." His mother didn't speak for a few moments and when she did her voice was strained and lifeless, the way it got when his father had done something she didn't like—what she usually called the "Bad news that follows your father around"—and uncertainty seemed to disturb the stale air of the cramped house.

"I thought you'd decided we'd wait until you had another job before we looked at cars," she said. "Can't hurt to look," his father smiled at him and shrugged, "besides, what kind of job am I going to get without a car? How will I get around to look for one?"

"I suppose, but—how will we pay for it?"

"Okay, I was teasing you. I'm not buying the car. Guy wants me to sell it and if I do maybe he'll take me on. I'll get a few hundred commission. Even if I don't find a sucker—that's dealer talk for a customer, by the way—we've got it for the weekend and I'm going to take us for a ride in the country."

"Oh, well," his mother softened, smiling faintly at his joke. She gazed from the open door at the sleek, shining Chevy. "We haven't taken the kids out in a long while."

It had grown dark when they reached the cottage, but no lights appeared to be on. "There's no one home," his mother said, sounding relieved.

"Don't be stupid, the cars are here so they've got to be around," his father said as he swung himself from the car and moved around to the trunk. He left their bags and pulled out a case of beer and a bottle of liquor. He went on up to the cottage door, waving for them to follow, so the boy's mother reluctantly stepped from the car, gathered the baby in her arms and gave the boy the baby's bag to carry. His father rapped on the door, grinning as if they'd already been welcomed in. Then he didn't wait but pushed the door open and went inside. "Hello," the boy heard him call. "Hey, you're here. Thought the place was deserted."

While his mother hesitated, lifting the baby to her shoulder and taking his sister's hand, the boy ran to join his father. He entered a large room where the darkness seemed to be deepened by a single kerosene lamp burning dimly on a small table in a far corner where his grandfather and another man sat playing cards. His grandfather leaned back, stiffly alert but saying nothing, and the boy was startled at the impression that the old man's eyes had suddenly flared with light, but it was only his glasses reflecting the lamp's yellow flame. It was the other man who reacted quickly, who jumped up in greeting as if he was the one his father's grin was meant for. "I'll be damned, it's your boy," he said loudly, as if the boy's grandfather might not recognize his own son, "and the kiddies and the beautiful Madame. Come in, come in."

"Hello, Froggy," his mother said shyly. "I hope we're not disturbing everyone."

"No, no, no," Froggy said, moving about to switch on several lamps before he pointed out the chairs and said, "Sit, sit, make yourself at home."

The boy felt a smile creeping onto his face as he watched the man with the funny name, surprised at how lively he was even though he was very short and shaped like a barrel. He patted the boy's head, then his sister's, tickled the baby, and then kissed the boy's mother on the cheek. He even squeezed his father's arm before he snatched the beer and liquor from him and crossed the room to a door which he swung wide to reveal a bright kitchen where the boy's grandmother and another woman sat drinking tea at a round table. "Look alive, Vangie," he shouted at the woman, who was as stout and rosy-faced as himself, "we've got company. Glasses all 'round."

Soon everyone except his sister and the baby, who'd been put in a bed, was seated at the table drinking and laughing at Froggy's funny remarks and stories. Even the boy's grandfather, to his great surprise, laughed loudly and, when he got the chance, told a few stories of his own.

Later, when he thought no one would hear, the boy whispered to his father, "Why does that man have such a funny name?" But his father answered loudly enough to draw everyone's attention. "So, you think Boutilier is a funny name, do you? Well he can't help that, it was his father's last name." The boy knew he was being teased and couldn't think what to say. "Oh, now wait a second," his father went on, "maybe you meant that Froggy is a funny name?" The boy's mother laid a hand on his father's arm and said, "Don't embarrass your son."

"We're only having a little fun," his father said, "and besides, he's right, Froggy is a funny name. Now why do you suppose they call him that? Is it because he has bulging eyes and hops around all the time, or...."

Froggy interrupted, "Ah, you are embarrassing the little fellow. Look, he's glowing like a firefly. I'll tell you, son, the simple reason I'm called Froggy. It's because I'm a Frenchman." He slapped the table and shouted some words the boy didn't understand, but which sounded like they might be swearing. Then everyone burst out laughing harder than ever. The boy understood this joke no more than he had the earlier stories, and his cheeks burned with the shameful idea that they were laughing at him. His father gave him a rough hug, which helped, and his mother led him to a big chair in the other room where he snuggled down and drifted in and out of sleep until she came back to tell him where he was to spend the night.

At first the boy wondered why his grandfather was the one who offered to lead him and his mother through the dark to the shed, but later he thought it was so he could warn him to leave his fishing stuff alone. It had been the first thing the boy noticed—drawn to the far wall where he stood on tiptoe and strained to reach one of the curious objects.

"What's this basket for?"

"Here," the old man pulled it away from him and put it on a higher hook. "You're spilling grass everywhere. It's a creel. Look, don't touch," he relented slightly, taking it down again to explain what it was. "See, a strap for carrying on your shoulder. A lid. A hole in the lid to drop in a fish. Put some grass in there, the fish don't get damaged, the sun doesn't dry them out. You understand?"

"And what's this?" Emboldened by curiosity, the boy stretched his arm up to try and lift a long canvas and leather case. The old man pushed his hand away in irritation. "Never mind. Why so nosy? These are my things. Got that? You don't touch them."

The boy had jumped back at the bark of the old man's voice and he looked round to make sure his mother was there. "It's for the fishing rods, isn't it? Don't worry, he's a good boy, he won't harm your precious...things," she said with a trace of anger. The old man scowled at both of them and left. The boy was relieved until his mother turned to him and said in the same hard angry voice, "Now don't for God's sake go poking about in your grandfather's fishing gear." She relented though, as she went about tucking him into the wide swaybacked bed, and the boy forgave her. It was his grandfather's fault anyway.

A clap of thunder woke him in the morning. He sat up and peered through the single small window. The green was awash with silver and gray, and the cottage seemed to be adrift in a blurry distance. He felt a mixture of excitement and fear and was just wondering what to do when his mother came out of the cottage and ran across the yard with her arms above her head to hold up an old army cape. He smiled as she burst into the shed, her cheeks red and gleaming damp. She blew her breath out in quick puffs that sounded a little like a panting dog. She dropped the cape in a wet heap and bounced down upon the end of the bed. She held out a paper bag and said, "I brought you a sandwich and some juice. I know you're always *starving* in the morning." They both laughed and he unwrapped the bag while she went on talking. "Your grandfather's in a foul mood this morning because he can't go fishing, so it might be for the best if you're not underfoot for a while. At least till he's had his coffee and found something in the paper to get worked up about." She was laughing again by the time she finished, so the boy knew she was making some sort of joke about his grandfather.

"Froggy has this little store with gas pumps and a section that's the post office and some groceries and candy and things just out on the road there. You can go over later if the rain lets up and Froggy says he'll give you a treat."

The boy nodded solemnly at this information, and his mother laughed again and tickled him as she said, "You eat and then colour or read for a while and then when you're dressed you can come to the cottage and play with your sisters." She stood up and draped the cape around her shoulders. She took a deep breath as she opened the door to go, as if she were about to plunge beneath the water and couldn't get any air till she reached the cottage. She'd pulled the door after her and he got up and opened it, but she'd already disappeared. He left it open while he sat on the bed and stared out at the heavy slanting rain and listened to it roaring against the roof of the shed.

Later, when the rain slowed to a steady mist, the boy went to the cottage. His father and Froggy were talking in the big room, something about men they'd known in the army, while his grandfather sat low in a big armchair with a paper held up so only his large-knuckled hands and his skinny legs were visible. His mother and grandmother and Froggy's wife were in the kitchen, washing dishes and baking. His sister was playing dolls in the bedroom and the baby was asleep again. The boy sat with drowsy patience, trying to work up the courage to ask Froggy about his store. In a short while, as if he'd read the boy's mind, the round little man bounced to his feet and rubbed his hands together enthusiastically. "Twelve o'clock, time for a drink. You pour," he said to the boy's father, "and this young man will help me get some mix from the store." He crossed the room and stood next to the boy. "Okay, partner, shake a leg." He went out and the boy followed.

As they walked the short distance to the store, Froggy asked his opinion on the weather and then, once they were inside the small overcrowded shop, went on talking to the boy as if he were an adult, showing him around, introducing him to the girl behind the counter, and asking how he liked things. "It's a fine little shop," the boy answered and Froggy laughed. Then he gave the boy a paper bag and began stuffing it with candy, chips, liquorice, and chocolate bars. When it was full, Froggy winked and said, "That's just for you. But maybe you don't tell your mama exactly how much you have, eh? In the shed underneath the bed is the place for that."

On the way back a question occurred to the boy. "Froggy, do you go fishing?"

"Me? Sure, I like to drown a few worms, but not like your Grandpa. He's a fool for it, tramping the woods every fine day he can. Why, you like to fish?"

"I don't know."

"Well, ask your Grandpa to take you. You can learn all his secret places and maybe drop a hint to old Froggy some time." He laughed at the boy's doubtful look. "Put your candy away and come back for a drink. You like a little rum?" He was laughing even harder as he went inside.

The boy had never considered going fishing, but now the idea seized him with the force of a desperate need. He hung about the cottage all afternoon, waiting for an opportunity to speak to his grandfather. None came. After a couple of drinks, they all gathered in the big room and began talking and laughing as they had the previous night. The boy repeated to himself again and again the few words he'd need to say: "Can you take me fishing?" But he was too shy to interrupt and increasingly certain his grandfather might not simply say no without adding something nasty. This thought frightened him in a way he couldn't understand. His grandfather wouldn't hurt him, not hit him anyway, because his mother and father wouldn't let him.

He grew drowsy with the repeating words and the sense of watchful anticipation buzzing inside his head like the flies lazily batting against the rain-streaked window panes. He waited. Froggy put a record on and danced with the boy's mother. His father danced too, with Froggy's wife, but his grandfather and grandmother stayed in their chairs, watching the others. They poured more drinks and talked some more. Sometimes everyone fell silent all at once and then they might look around at each other and laugh out loud at nothing.

The boy didn't follow most of the conversation except to notice that they grew louder as the afternoon wore on, and the stories and laughter got mixed in with more and more arguing. It was the men mostly who did that, and it seemed to be about some things the government was doing. The boy found it curious that they found the stories about the army, and even the war, so funny, but got mad and red-faced over these government things.

He lost hope of speaking to his grandfather and concentrated on wishing his mother would ask him what he wanted to do with himself. "Go fishing," he'd shout. He was bored and half asleep in the big soft chair when an outburst between his father and grandfather startled him into attention. Without his noticing, his father had moved across the room next to the old man, and now he'd jumped up and hurried into the kitchen. Everyone else looked as confused as the boy felt. His mother went into the kitchen too, and in a moment the boy followed, though he stayed just inside the door.

"Did you ask him?" his mother said.

"Oh, I asked him," his father said with his teeth clamped tight, "I goddamn asked him."

"What did he say that…?"

"He didn't say anything."

"He must…what were you arguing about?" His mother had put her hand on his father's shoulder, but he didn't turn around.

"He just had to give me his lecture on the used-car business. He's an expert on it, did you know that? An expert, like he is about everything else. A good way to lose your shirt, he says. A waste of time, he says. Oh I know about that…a goddamn waste of time talking to him, I said. We might as well get out of here now."

"No, hon, it's late and you—we've been drinking. We'll have to stay the night."

"Momma," the boy found himself saying, though he hadn't meant to speak, and his mother looked at him like she might not know who he was. "Is Papa upset?"

"Papa's fine. Why don't you go out and draw for a while and I'll call you for supper."

The boy left with his head down, not wanting to look at anyone, feeling as if he'd done something wrong. In the shed he crawled across the bed and wedged himself into the corner against the wall. He stared vacantly at the opposite wall until it occurred to him a long time had passed, and then he thought resentfully that he'd been forgotten. He hadn't decided what to do when a moment later the door swung open and his grandfather walked in. "Savin' the lights are you?" He tugged the string of the overhead bulb and went to the gear on the wall to take down a dark wooden box held closed by brass hooks. He set it on the bed, opened it, and took something out. It was too small for the boy to see in the old man's cupped hand.

"What's that?" The boy shifted onto his knees and stretched forward in an effort to see.

"Flies," his grandfather said, flattening his hand so the boy could see three small hooks with brightly coloured thread, bits of fur, and feathers tied to them They weren't flies at all. "They attract the fish, trout mostly around here," the old man said, but seeing the skeptical twist of the boy's mouth, he smiled faintly and added, "They're used instead of worms. I made them myself. You know anything about fishing? Your dad take you?"

The boy shook his head. "No, but I'd like to go fishing...sometime." He'd said it as simply as that, the words tumbling out before he'd had a chance to think twice about asking the old man for anything.

The old man seemed startled. "Oh, now, I don't know," he spoke with a thoughtful frown. "Tomorrow may be fine, so I'd be going out early. If so...well if your father came along he could bring you. I suppose that would be okay." He put the box back on its hook and stepped outside, then leaned back in and said, "Oh, I'm supposed to tell you supper is ready."

The boy watched his grandfather cross the yard, hiking his pants as he went, then smoothing back his cropped white hair, a gesture exactly like the boy's papa often made. He stood on the bed and reached out to stroke each piece of fishing gear once before he hopped down and ran to tell his mother. Tomorrow!

The sun was a large red ball snared in the treetops when his grandfather came to get him. The old man looked surprised to find him ready, dressed and sitting on the edge of the bed. The boy had been waiting since the air in the shed began to glow with the first dawn light, and he'd slept little anyway, nestled under the blankets while confused images of their coming expedition crowded his head. The old man had hesitated under the boy's expectant gaze. Finally he said, "You really think you'd like to go fishing, eh? All right, come on."

While his grandfather took down his gear, the boy waited on the step, hoping he might be asked to carry something. But the old man simply told him to get in the car, then stored everything in the trunk and went back to the cottage for their lunch.

The boy had settled into the back seat, where he always rode unless he was alone with his father, but when his grandfather slid behind the wheel he said, without looking at him, "You might as well ride shotgun." As he scrambled over the seat, the boy looked about for his father but saw no sign of him.

As the car sped along the gravel road, the boy craned his neck to peer at the rushing canopy of leaves, the occasional glimpse of open fields and distant houses, and as they came to the crests of hills, the blue sparkling lake.

Everything still glistened wet from the rain, but the sun rose quickly to the east beyond the lake, and soon steam rose everywhere and slipped like thin fingers of cloud across the bright expanse of the car's hood.

It was the boy's grandfather who broke the silence. "Your father chickened out. He's got a *headache*. Wonder how he got that? So that's why it's just the two of us. Your mother says you'd be disappointed if I don't take you. You know about that, being disappointed? It's something you get used to, but I suppose you don't need to start so young." The old man spoke in a frank conversational tone which surprised the boy because it sounded as if his grandfather were talking to another adult. The boy said nothing, just waited and wondered what it would be like to hold a fish in his hands.

His grandfather eventually pulled onto the side of the road next to a narrow bridge which crossed a brook that looked just like the seven or eight they'd already passed by. There'd been no talk for a while and now the old man just climbed from the car with a low groan and stood stretching his arms over his head before going round to the trunk. He pulled on a pair of rubber boots which were so long that even with the tops folded down several times they came over his knees. He gave the boy a smaller pair. "Put these on. They should just about fit. They belonged to your Aunt Mary. You remember her? No? No, I suppose she moved away when you were a baby. Up in Toronto now. Been back a couple of times, I guess."

The boy listened carefully, unsure what he was being told exactly, but thinking that this new talkative grandfather might be better than the sour, quiet one he was used to. But the old man clamped his mouth shut again, gathered the fishing gear, and made his way through the steep ditch to the edge of the brush which grew along the stream and against the dark treeline. "Come on," was all he said as he began to shoulder his way into the dense alders.

The boots were too large for the boy's small feet and he had to lift his knees at just the right angle to keep them from sliding off. The mud sucked at them too, so he had to grip the boot top before lifting his foot from the sticky clay. Once he made it out of the ditch it was better because he could shuffle through the tall weeds. They were heavy with water though, and by the time he reached the alders, his pants were soaked. Then, each time he touched an alder branch, water rained down so his jacket and shirt were drenched too when he emerged under the first spruce trees. His grandfather had stopped a dozen steps further on, but when he saw the boy appear, he moved on quickly into the woods. The boy tried to close the distance between them but the cumbersome boots slowed him too much, and he had to keep his eyes down or risk tripping over the moss-covered rocks and exposed roots. A number of times, when he glanced up to make sure of his direction, his grandfather had disappeared and he felt a brief stab of panic. But then he'd see the old man emerge from behind a tree or squatting impatiently in the shadows, waiting for the boy, though only until he knew he'd been spotted, when he'd charge off again. The boy wasn't frightened exactly, but he felt as if a host of unknown feelings were about to overrun his small body.

It was hot, and the damp clothing added a steamy weight to the burden of the large boots. And then the flies found him, tiny black ones biting his hands and neck and face and sticking to the sweat around his eyes. His thoughts about fishing and the excited expectation of handling his grandfather's fishing gear had faded, and his heart thumped in his ears with echoes of anger and resentment. Fishing was no fun. And he didn't like the old man even one little bit.

His senses felt dulled the way they were just before he fell asleep at night. He thought suddenly of the children who were taken into the woods and abandoned. But that was only a story his mother had read to him. His grandfather wouldn't do that. He wanted to cry, but then even that feeling seemed to be located at a distance outside of himself. He stumbled and fell hard, and when he stood up his grandfather was beside him.

"You ready to fish?"

"I want to go home," the boy said just above a whisper.

His grandfather looked down at him for a time, and then pointed back at the darkly patterned woods they'd come through. "Go ahead. It's that way."

"But I'll get lost."

"Now you're catching on," the old man said as he turned away and went on through the trees. The boy found his tears now, felt them stinging the corners of his eyes, but he also felt an unfamiliar urge to resist the old man's meanness. He pulled off the heavy boots and tucked them under an arm. In sock feet he could run across the thick moss on the rocks and across the leaf-thickened hollows between the tangled roots. Ignoring the occasional pinch of sharp rocks and branches, he quickly caught up to his grandfather.

The old man was standing in a small clearing where a tiny brook ran into the bigger one. There was a curl of gravel where he'd placed the boxes, creel and cases. The water didn't rush past here, twisting and splashing among large stones, but moved slowly over the dark depth of a pool created by a pair of great logs which had fallen and dammed the stream.

The boy sank down onto the damp, sandy gravel and pulled on his boots while he watched his grandfather. He'd crouched to open the long canvas and leather case and pulled out the sections of a long rod which he fitted together. He put a reel on the thickest end above a cork handle and then took out a short rod with a reel already attached. He handed this to the boy and put a worm on the hook at the end of the line. He told the boy to sit on a boulder at the edge of the pool and showed him how to put the line out in the water.

"Now," he said, his voice pitched low so he wouldn't alert the fish, "you just wait. If something tugs on the line you just wait a minute till the hook sets, then start winding this handle on the reel. Got that?"

The boy nodded, though he'd grown vague and disinterested in the process, his thoughts fixed instead on his discomfort at the heat and the itching fly bites. He could see fish in the water below him, however, small brown ones which shone with specks of light and colour when they darted from the shadows, which held his attention for a while. When he looked up again, he saw his grandfather was standing out in the pool, his boots rolled up to his hips so the water couldn't get in. He kept flicking his rod back and forth so the line whipped through the air, shimmering like light itself, to drop one of the tiny feathered hooks into the far side of the pool. In a moment he'd begun again, and the boy watched through squinted eyes, following the line's snaking passage, back and forth, back and forth, as his head drooped sleepily and his own rod dipped into the water.

He woke to a splash and the icy rush of water running into his boots and over his scrabbling legs.

ANGLERS

His grandfather's hands grasped him roughly, yanked him into the air. He felt a wrench of terror as he hung inches away from the ruddy lined face, the red-rimmed eyes, the yellowed teeth clenched within the grimacing mouth. "You little bugger!" He set him down on the gravel and the boy stared sheepishly at his soggy knees, hearing the clatter and rasp of the gear being stowed away, too embarrassed to look at the old man.

With the various straps slung round his shoulders, the old man lifted the boy into his arms and carried him across the logs and into the brush and trees on the other side. In a moment they broke into sunshine and he set the boy down on the edge of the road. They were only a couple of hundred feet from the car. For just an instant the boy wondered why they'd had to walk so far through the woods, then he hurried after his grandfather and climbed into the back seat where the old man had impatiently flung all the gear.

"My god, what happened?" his mother said, her tone of alarm releasing in him a confused sense of self-pity, and the boy's face flushed with heat as the first tears blurred his eyes and ran scalding down his cheeks.

His mother snatched him up almost as roughly as his grandfather had, but with the compassionate intent of rescuing him from an ordeal he'd already passed through. The sloshing boots slid from his feet and, as he was rushed into the cottage, he heard his grandfather complaining, "He frightened every goddamn trout in the county is what happened."

Inside the door, his mother halted for a fraction of a second. "He's only a child, how...how could you possibly...," she cried out with a desperation which frightened the boy more than his experience in the woods.

"That's right," the old man crowed in hoarse triumph, "only a child and he had no business out there. Wipe his arse for him. Baby him until he's just like his father."

The boy's mother stood him on the toilet seat and stripped off the wet clothing. In fascination he watched himself in the mirror.

His face was streaked with dirt and tears, puffy with crying and fly bites which were crusted with blood, here and there smeared into tiny red stars where he'd rubbed at them. His mother ran water in the sink. Too hot. Then, more roughly than she intended, she scrubbed his face and hands with a cloth till his skin was pink and gleaming, as if she were trying to rub away something more than a few dried trickles of blood. As she inspected him, she asked in a shaky voice, "Oh, what did he do to you, baby?"

"He called me a little bugger," the boy whispered. "I frightened all the fish, even the big ones," he added more firmly, with a sort of startled pride.

Her face darkened. She lifted him again and, against his protests that he didn't have any clothes on, carried him out into the yard toward the shed. The old man emerged from the small building when they were about mid-way there and she put him down. "Go get dressed and put your things in your bag, we're leaving when your father gets back."

He hurried past the old man who watched him with amusement.

As the boy dressed, he eyed the fishing gear which hung on the wall as if it had never left there, as if the morning had been just a dream. He heard his mother speaking loudly outside. She was saying something about the boy's father, and it was only then he realized he hadn't seen him since they'd come back. "He went with Froggy to the bootlegger's for more beer. But don't worry, he won't be staying to drink it. We're leaving. Okay? Happy now?"

"Christ, almighty. Why is everything such a melodrama with you people? Here, take this. Maybe it'll take the knot out of your face."

The boy watched his grandfather hold a piece of paper out to his mother. She took it slowly, staring at it like she didn't know what to do with it.

"What's this?"

"A cheque. The money you asked for."

"A cheque made out to me...why? I didn't ask for this. You shame your own son and now you shame me because you know I can't refuse it. What will he think? But you know, don't you? You know exactly how to hurt him."

"So cash it and give him the money...hell, let's not make a big deal out of it."

"Why do you go out of your way to hurt him, to humiliate him?" his mother asked, her voice rising to a shrill note. The boy thought she was going to cry and he backed into the shed. But he could still hear them.

"He's unreliable. He's weak. You don't know how often I've tried to help him. He won't listen to my advice. No, thinks he knows better. And he's ten times worse since the war. He needs to be wakened up. I told you ten years ago...."

"Yes you did, and you made sure he knew, and you make sure he knows how you despise him, how you think he's weak and a liar. You're a nasty, bitter man who thinks everyone else has to suffer...."

"Jesus woman, I just want him to do what's right. Anything I ever said was for your benefit, to try and get you to see what you were in for. But you turned out to be as blind and stubborn as him."

"You won't stop, will you? You'll go right on hurting him no matter what he does, no matter how much he tries to win your approval. I just pray he sees that your help is no help."

They went on and on and the boy couldn't understand what they were arguing about. Except he knew his grandfather had hurt his father somehow. That didn't surprise him. He saw the old man again towering over him in the woods. Heard him say, "Now you're catching on." The boy filled with a bitterness toward the old man, a dark feeling he couldn't name.

He acted then as if his body had run ahead of his thoughts, and he watched from outside himself with mute astonishment. Leaning from the edge of the bed and stretching as far as he could, he was able to lift each piece of fishing gear from its hook and drop it onto the floor. He arranged them neatly just inside the door, which he pushed closed, and stood wondering what he intended, but only for a moment because his hands moved as if they had a plan of their own. They drew the three sections of the long fishing rod from the stiff canvas and leather case. He handled them carefully, flexed the lightest of the three, let it whip out straight again. He dropped it along with the middle one on the shed floor. The butt section—with the cork handgrip and the neat sliding sections which would hold the gimmicky reel in place—dangling from his right hand, he peered cautiously through the grimy glass of the single small window to check that his mother and grandfather were still preoccupied. They'd know he'd done it, he wanted them to, but his stomach clenched sickly at the thought of being caught in the act.

Carefully, he placed the three pieces of the rod together on the floor and stepped on them with his left foot, then grasped the wider ends with both hands and bent them upwards. They were fibreglass, he thought, and they were meant to bend easily without snapping. But they had to have a breaking point and he bent them into a deep trembling u-shape before he began with the weight of his body as much as his slight, shaking arms, to force them slowly back down upon themselves.

Tim Vassallo

Chainsaw

It was Sunday afternoon when I got the call. There had been a reprieve from the slow but steady trudge towards winter, and I was trying to get all the piles of raked leaves into one big pile while the warm wind kept the snow away. I was awkwardly trying to use the rake as a shovel to gather the leaves and shove them into one of those clownish large garden trash bags, when my daughter screamed from the back step.

"Something has happened to Gramps. He fell or something. They need you...."

Her voice was shrill and it rang in my ears as I ran toward the house. I don't know what I did with the bag or the rake but I was off across the backyard before the screen door shut. When I got to the house my wife and daughter were standing there with one holding the car keys and the other holding my jacket. I was unaware of the details; that didn't seem to matter at the time.

My father has lived in his family's old house since his mother passed away—and that was before I was born. The house is a huge two-storey with four full-sized dormers on the front looking across the valley below. I lived in that house for eighteen years, and it was always "The Family House."

And that meant the whole family.

During some summers every spare foot was occupied by cousins of some sort or another. They seemed to love coming "Home," as they all called it, even though some had never been here before. But that's the way the old fella liked it.

He used to tell us stories about the old days, when the farm was a working farm and when the lumber mill still ran full bore during the spring and fall, or when the only words you would hear would be in Gaelic.

When I got to the farm I was unable to remember the reason for my trip. The clouds were thin ribbons above the hills that rolled off towards the water, and I scanned the entire horizon before the thought of Dad came rolling back to me.

When I entered the house I was met by that familiar mixture of heat and strong tea. The wood stove was doing its job, making the kitchen and pantry nearly unbearably hot. That was a good sign because at least he was able to keep the stove going; he couldn't be in too bad a shape. I had left in such a hurry I didn't think to ask my wife or daughter if they knew what had happened. I thought I heard them say that the neighbour had called, but the rest was lost on me. I called out and heard something and realized he was probably in the front room.

"What the hell happened to you? What were you doing?"

My father is sitting up with his legs out before him on a kitchen chair, and he has a nasty gash above his right eye. There are deep scratches down both cheeks and a small cut on his thick neck. I move slowly over to where he sits without taking my eyes off him. He just shrugged his shoulder and smiled at me with his toothless mouth, while his teeth smiled from the TV tray beside the chair.

"I guess I didn't tie the knot tight enough. Shoulda went to scouts, wha?" He laughed.

In a slow, calm voice I asked, "What do you mean? What were you doing with a rope?"

"I was trying to put the chainsaw to a tree that's been bothering me for the longest time."

He broke my stare with a wave of his teacup, and I grabbed the cup and went to fill it for him.

In the pantry I looked out the small window he had put in years ago at my mother's request, so she could look down over the bank at the side of the house. I could see a pile of wood at the base of the hill, and some rope. I pushed myself up on the counter and saw where the old loon had tied the rope onto the pole that used to hold the birdfeeder.

He had cut down that old gnarled birch that grew uglier each year. And because it was on the side that was unseen from the road and from almost every window in the house, *I* figured that it should just keep growing uglier and uglier every year. Dad hadn't mentioned his plan, but that means nothing. He would rather admit to being wrong about something than admit something bothered him.

Back in the front room my father is asleep in his chair. His toothless mouth looks like that of a baby and not an eighty-two-year-old crazy bugger. I watch him for less than a minute, until the clock chimes three. He wakes up slowly and tries to get out of the chair, forgetting about his sore head, but sits back down when he realizes how much it hurts. I hand him the cup of tea and he places the cup next to his teeth on the TV table, watching steam curling up from the cup until the tea cools.

"Are there any sweets out there in the pantry? I think Widow MacIsaac from up the road sent some squares over on Friday." He didn't look up at all, trying to take a sip of tea.

When I came back with the squares on an old china plate he was trying to regain his balance, using the arm of the chair for support. He smiled at me and tried to get me off the topic that was hanging in the air like the smell of tea and wood heat.

He asked me if I had seen the game on TV, as if there was only one game on last night; now there are ten or more hockey games on TV on any given night during the season. He couldn't follow much of what was happening in hockey these days with all the expansion teams and crazy salaries, but he would watch every Saturday as if by nature and not by choice. After going on about some "stupid" call by some "thick" ref, he sat back down. I could tell he didn't have his balance back yet. He was trapped and could not make an excuse to get away from me and the inevitable.

"Dad, what were you doing out beside the house—with the rope and the chainsaw?"

He said nothing and just stared out the window beside him, the window that gives up the best view of the valley and all the colours between here and the horizon.

"Listen Dad, if you need stuff like that done, just call me and I'll come out to help." I offered the assistance trying not to embarrass him.

He smiled. "Guess I'll calls you when I need to take a piss now, eh?"

"Come on Dad, you're over eighty years old and…." I stopped because the smile was instantly erased from his face.

He just sat there like an old coat slumped into the chair. His eyes were wet and he was rubbing his hands together.

I went out to the shed beside the house where he kept all his tools. The old barn had burned down three summers ago; it caught during a fire he had accidentally let get out of control while burning slash. The whole building was nearly gone by the time the volunteer fire department arrived. My dad said that the boys were the best around and hadn't lost a foundation yet.

I found his chainsaw on the concrete floor underneath the workbench. On the wall near the bench hung the letter from the Department of Highways thanking him for his forty-six years of service and the fine work he had done. The letter was signed in one of those dramatic, flowing autographs and he had placed it in a handmade frame. I took it off the wall and held it in my hands.

I remembered those nights when the snow would start and he, without a word, would go to the drying room and get his winter coveralls and his heavy department-issued canvas coat. He would tie up his boots before he was ready to go and we could hear him clomping from anywhere in the house. I was always proud of him and how big he was and how much fun he was to be around. He was just one of those guys.

The chainsaw was still warm and there was a scraggly piece of yellow nylon rope tied around the handle. I could only imagine the scene: Dad with the rope and a chainsaw hanging over the hill, holding on by what?

Chainsaw

I grabbed the chainsaw and walked quickly out to the car. I laid it down on the ground and fumbled in my jacket pocket for my keys. I was far more lost than my keys.

The door opened at the side of the house and my father was standing in the doorway nearly filling the entire frame. He just stood there staring at me. I couldn't make eye contact with him. He stared straight at me as if to dare me to look back. I placed the chainsaw in the trunk and I walked, head down, towards the side of the house. I stood at the top of the hill, where it runs from the side of the house down to the brook. I was looking down on the small pile of wood that used to be the offending tree.

I tried to descend the steep incline without going "ass over tea kettle," a feat made impossible by the wet leaves that the old tree had shed before its demise. And then I was on my back, out of control, and sliding down the length of the hill.

As I tried to pick myself up off the cold ground, there stood my father at the top of the hill, laughing so hard that he had to cough up in his handkerchief, which he then folded into a small square and placed back in his pants pocket. He was waving at me as if I couldn't see him; the smile on his face was as wide as the sky.

"Do ya need a hand down there, old man, or will you be all right on your own?" He was leaning up against the house and was shaking his head back and forth in mock disgust.

I got to my feet and realized that the entire old tree was now a neat pile of wrinkled logs cut the perfect size for the wood stove.

I yelled up the hill. "How the hell did you get these cut and piled after you fell?"

"Well, boy, what the frig was I gonna do? I was already down there anyways."

I gave him another good show as I tried to climb the hill, my arms flailing for balance as my feet slid out from beneath me, again and again. I finally made it to the house but he had slipped off to the side door.

He was standing in the middle of the kitchen facing the big

window next to the table. He was in his undershirt now, sweating from the heat of the stove, his plaid work shirt over the chair. He didn't say much to me as I milled about the house checking up on things before I left. I tried to get his mind off the events of the day by asking him what he wanted for Christmas.

"I guess a chainsaw is outta the question, wha?"

I didn't respond. I checked the stove and brought some wood up from the cellar. As I made for the door, I cleared my throat. Then I offered one last apology.

"This isn't easy for me, you know. You're my father; I don't like telling you what to do."

There was no reply until I touched the doorknob.

"Yeah, and it ain't easy for me either, but you'll be here someday and this'll happen to you. Then you'll know how I felt. It don't matter about right and wrong. It's all wrong at my age."

I drove my car down the rough gravel road that leads back out to the highway. As I turned onto the blacktop I thought back to the day we took his ladder away after he nearly fell off the roof while checking the stovepipe. He was kicking the dirt like a penned horse while we tied the ladder onto the roof of the car. He never did say a word or raise a stink. He just watched me as I drove away. I will always remember the stone-faced stare in my rear-view mirror.

This was the thought that followed me all the way back to my house. I just couldn't shake that memory from my head. As I pulled into my driveway every room was lit up against the evening's murky sky. I sat in the car thinking about the old man and his eighty-two years on this earth.

Everything serves some purpose or other, even that ugly old tree that he cut down. Then all I could think about was the neat pile of logs at the bottom of the hill.

Charlotte Musial

Old, Young Love

"Look at it this way," Henri says, lifting the coffee cup to his lips. "You have nothing to lose. Right?"

I study the man sitting opposite me in the mid-morning coffee shop. A cross between Peter Gzowski and Peter O'Toole—with the former's plummy voice, disheveled air, and warm intelligence, and the latter's jewel-blue eyes—Henri still has the power to fascinate. I can only imagine how he'd looked when he'd married his wife, Margaret, fifty years ago. It's easy to see, despite his physical frailty, why women of a certain age—indeed, any age—might still succumb to his charms. Caught in the beam of those eyes, seduced by that voice, one quite forgets the fingers, gnarled and twisted like old tree roots around the cup, and the fragile chest that rises and falls with what one hopes isn't his second-last breath. "Right?" he says again.

"Right," I say, shifting my gaze to the shop door that faces Main Street where a young couple has just entered, stamping their feet and brushing snowflakes off each other's shoulders. He wears a navy blue jacket, jeans, and ski boots; she, a fluorescent pink jacket, matching pants, and knee-high black boots. Both pairs of young cheeks glow, and both pairs of eyes sparkle. They pull toques off their heads, their hair crackling—poster children for youth and health and vitality. Henri and I, on the other hand, are poster children for "been there, done that." I watch them order two decafs, and then I look back at Henri.

"Well, you're right." I shrug. "Nothing to lose. Except...." I pause, groping for words.

"Except?"

"Well, the thing is, I feel that I do. Maybe. Have something to lose."

"And what can that be?" Henri fusses with the crumbs of his bagel. Veins like tributaries meander across the back of his hand.

"Well, that's what I haven't figured out yet. It's just a feeling. Vague."

"How long did you say since you saw this chap?" Henri uses words like "chap" and "unseemly," a trait of his I treasure.

"Years. Not since three years after high school."

"And you still remember him?" Henri's grizzled eyebrows rise. "Still carrying the torch?"

I consider the cliché. Despite some thirty years between Henri and me, I understand "carrying the torch." Am I? Time hasn't erased my young love. So many images and memories of Jaime.

"Hey, Vonnie," Henri says, "you still with me?"

My cheeks flush. "Here's the thing, Henri," I say. "It all happened decades ago."

I shrug and drain the tepid coffee from my cup, trying to appear nonchalant. Then, placing my empty mug on the table between us, I immediately undermine my credibility by adding, "But I still remember."

Henri is quiet for a moment. "Don't we all," he murmurs, peering past me and into another time and place. Then, "So go for it. See if you can find him and find out what happened. Why he lost touch." He shifts in his seat, searches his pockets for a tip. "Seems to me that's a valid thing to do, given that you're sure he felt the same about you?"

"Yes. I was sure then, and I still am."

"There you go, then." My companion levers himself to his feet and drops a loonie on the table.

"My treat," he says, picking up the cheque. I watch him approach the cash register, the movement of each limb so slow that it resembles time-lapse photography. The cashier waits patiently while Henri rummages again in pockets for change, and then we leave the café and make our way back to our apartments, two blocks away.

Old, Young Love

Icy wind slices through my jacket and pants, tosses my hair into a mess of brown frizz. I curse the chic boots, my one concession to fashion, and wish I'd worn my safer flats. Wish I didn't hate ugly shoes.

Some fifteen minutes later, during which Henri, with the speed of continental drift, skirts icy patches and February snow banks, we arrive at the back porch of the Victorian house where we've occupied the two ground-floor apartments for the past three years. In that time, we've become close companions, as unlikely as that seems to our friends and acquaintances. Though why that should surprise, when we're all past the age of seeking soul mates and alter egos, remains unclear. Despite others' skepticism, Henri and I have an understanding, and we're happy with it.

Another thing we share besides the first floor, the view of the harbour, the landlord, and our Zodiac sign, is a calico cat.

An enchanting vixen who, with her vivid orange, white, and black coat and wicked black patch over one eye, declared me her subject the first time she preceded me, with her entitled air, into my apartment. I'd christened her "The Empress" on the spot. Since that day in October, she'd alternated between Henri and me, endowing each of us with her presence, depending on her mood. Henri refuses to acknowledge her as female and stubbornly refers to her as he, his, or him. Nothing I say—nor the evidence—can dissuade him, so I consider it a foible and let it rest. I know that, despite this blind spot, Henri still has a healthy interest in gender.

Now, as we unlock our separate doors in the dimly lit hall, Henri says, "Google your chap. If he's done anything noteworthy, he'll be there."

"I already have," I say, thinking how impossible it is to imagine Jaime *not* doing noteworthy things. "Ten thousand hits, all dead ends."

"Then Google someone who might remember him." Henri executes a wobbly salute before closing his door. "See you in the morning," he says, "same time."

"You're on."

LOCAL HERO

"By the way, Vonnie," he says, opening his door again, "you look very fetching today." He winks and then closes his door for good this time.

The Empress sashays into my apartment as if she knows that Henri will shortly be practicing his fiddle, a cacophony of exercises and scales that unnerves her and me as violently as bagpipes before breakfast.

During my solitary lunch, and later between phone calls to my real estate clients, I consider Henri's suggestion to try Google again. Semi-retired for a year, I love my snug apartment, my option to work from home, my flexible schedule, my relationship with Henri. My kids are settled; my ex is occupied. In short, everything about my current life situation pleases me.

All of which leaves ample time to obsess about my old, young love.

After the evening news, I page through my oldest photo album and find my high-school prom pictures. For several minutes I study my favourite. In it, Jaime wears a borrowed white sport coat and a pink carnation. His dark hair is slicked back; his dark eyes focus on me. I wear a frilly white gown, a rose corsage pinned at the shoulder, and a trailing pink ribbon in my hair. I smile at Jaime.

Who took that picture? Tuning out the monotonous fiddle exercises from across the hall, petting The Empress who sits melting in my lap, I concentrate. Jaime's best friend, Matthew? Matthew's date, Valerie? Of course! Valerie Kanova, prom queen, who had double-dated that night with Matthew and Jaime and me, and whom I hadn't heard from—or of—in years.

I dump The Empress off my lap and boot up my computer. My hope of finding Valerie on line is slim, but she was on the fast track to success before "fast track" was in anyone's lexicon, and if anyone from my past can update me, it's Valerie. She'd always known what was going on. Never mind that I'd have to apologize for my prolonged silence; after all, she'd been silent for years, too, and we'd never been best friends to begin with. We'd had Jaime and Matthew in common, period.

I type "Valerie Kanova" in Google. A couple of forays later, I click on *Vali's Fashion Hall of Fame*; her website fairly crackles with snappy references to the awards she's won for fashion design.

After the preliminaries (>saw your site, been home lately?<) I approach the topic of our past, first using a few red herrings to camouflage my mission. Minutes later, I come to it: Does she remember prom night and Jaime?

To my surprise, she's reading her email as I write, and she immediately replies. >Jaime? Oh yes, of course I remember him, dear. Heard he got married, divorced, remarried, re-divorced, and died out west of an aortic aneurysm two years ago. Seems he was childless and virtually friendless. Alcohol problem. So sad. Why? You still carrying the torch? Ha.<

>Not me< I reply. >Just curious<

I ask Valerie to let me know of any contacts she's kept over the years, wish her good luck and sign off.

Shaken, I stand at my living room window and stare blindly at the harbour, my mind filled with images of Jaime. Reflected by the night, a stranger stares back at me. Her face is lined. Her silver-streaked hair has lost its luster, her body its youthful definition. Would Jaime have recognized me now? Would he have remembered the August day we said goodbye, the day our promises fell, on that windy shore, like litanies from our salty lips?

I'd waited too long to find out. With his dying, Jaime took a chunk of my history. While he was alive, his memories of me lived—memories shared by no one else, not even by me, for I couldn't recall my young self half as clearly as I did the young him.

Outside, the lights of the city encircle the arm of the harbour like a bracelet, and I become aware that, across the hall, Henri is no longer practising. He's abandoned scales and exercises, jigs and reels. Silence. Then I hear his fiddle again. The sublime melody of Jerry Holland's "My Lily" drifts, as it does most evenings at the end of his practice, across the dimly lit hall that separates our apartments. "My Lily" is Henri's *pièce de résistance*, but I've never heard him play it as hauntingly as he does tonight. Each silvery note, each exquisite phrase, belies the stiffness of arthritic fingers, the rigidity of strings and bow, and emanates not from the instrument but from some ethereal place within Henri himself.

When the last note fades, I turn away from the window, and The Empress and I go to bed.

I lie awake until dawn. I identify my loss, face my deepest regret about the past: Jaime and I had been sweethearts; we'd been soul mates; we'd been friends. But we hadn't been lovers. We'd been true to the rules of the time, rules we'd been taught would ensure our futures, and we'd been false to ourselves.

I arise in time to prepare, as is our tradition, Sunday breakfast for The Empress and for Henri and myself. Promptly at nine o'clock, just as the coffee gasps its last and I transfer the sizzling bacon to the warm oven, Henri gently taps on my door.

The Empress follows me as I open it and, as Henri steps gingerly over the threshold, she greets him by gliding around his ankles as if he were her best buddy.

"So this is where he's been all night," Henri says, picking her up and burying his nose in her immaculate fur. "Shame on you," he mumbles into her neck. "I was all alone last night, hoping you'd come to visit. When you didn't, I thought you must be out philandering like any self-respecting tom."

He ambles over to the table, which I'd set with yellow place mats, blue napkins, and lighted candles in defiance of the dreary February day.

The Empress yawns widely and wiggles out of Henri's arms, then claims her favourite corner on my sofa where she begins her Sunday morning toilette, which seems to be even more scrupulous than her meticulous weekday ablutions. For a moment, we silently watch the pink tongue slide between each pair of spread toes and then move on to the white bib under her chin. Satisfied with the bib, she returns to her toes and begins spreading and washing anew.

Henri sighs. "You might be right," he concedes. "Maybe he is a girl. No tom I've known was ever concerned enough with hygiene to do it all twice."

I hide a smile.

For the next fifteen minutes, Henri and I savour salty bacon, fried eggs, buttery toast, and honest-to-God coffee. Then, while he spreads raspberry jelly on a warm bran muffin, he raises those blue eyes to mine and says, "So. Did you find anything out?"

I refill his coffee cup. "I did."

"Well...tell me."

"I will in a minute," I say, capturing The Empress and cuddling her on my lap. "But first," I say, sneaking her a morsel of bacon and passing Henri the cream, "tell me about your Lily."

Joyce Rankin

A Wagon Load

THE STOVE WAS ALREADY HOT, the water in the kettle singing, and the teapot filled with hot strong tea. Papa and the boys had tea, and we had glasses of milk. It is the Saturday of the Thanksgiving weekend, and this is the day to pick the potatoes. In this, everyone helps, because there are two big plots, and we need the potatoes to get us through the winter. Yesterday Papa walked the drills pulling tops off the potato plants and piling them at the corners of the plot, making ready for today.

Mother has been up for hours. There is porridge in bowls and pots bubbling on the stove. Through the window I see a row of sheets and towels flap on the line in the October wind, colours bright in the strong clear light. She stands behind me while I spoon porridge into my mouth, brushes my long hair, and her quick fingers make neat braids and slip elastics onto the ends.

"Try and stay a little bit clean," she says, and my sister and I look at each other across our bowls. Isn't that half the fun, digging in the earth and not having to stay clean?

Alex Joe and James get up from the table to walk back to the field while Papa finishes his tea. The day is fine and the walk is short, and maybe they are thinking of last Saturday when they were driving the wagon with a load of wood and a crowd of their friends passed in a car and blew the horn. But we are younger and we are thrilled to ride on the wagon with Papa, back to the field we call up-across-the-road.

When we get to the field, the boys are there and they lift the plough down from the wagon. They disconnect the harness from the wagon and hook up to the plough. Papa positions the blade.

A Wagon Load

With James driving the horses and Father steering the plough, the gleaming blade skims expertly along the sides of the drills, nosing its way underneath the roots of the plants and overturning them to expose the pale round potatoes in the crumbling dark soil.

Along the drills they go, in straight lines and patterns. We walk after with buckets, stooping to pick up the potatoes, the loamy smell of earth contrasting with the sharp autumn scent of impending winter. Digging in with our fingers when we see rounded shapes and lighter brown potato flesh in what looked like a lump of earth, we pluck the potatoes from the places where they have been hiding all summer. Their skins camouflage them in the brown earth, but the white flesh of the broken ones gleams against the matte darkness. The broken ones we fling into the field for the cows to graze on later—once the skin is broken they're apt to rot and infect the others if piled together in the cellar.

As each bucket is filled we carry it to the wagon, where the tailgate has been slid into its slot at the end to make a secure box for cargo. We dump in the potatoes and go back for more. When the wagon is full, the boys unhitch the horses from the plough and lead them to the shallow banks of the river, where they stretch their necks and dip their mouths into the cold water to drink. Then they hitch them back to the wagon and Papa climbs onto the seat.

We are heading home for the dinner Mother will have waiting. She will time it so that when she sees the wagon turn in at the end of the lane she pushes the pot of dinner and the kettle from the warm side-burner to the hottest part of the stove.

Papa and the boys pull up to the house and back the wagon around. They set the wooden chute through the open window and into the cellar bins with the wooden walls and packed earth floor, and with their hands—so as not to tear the skins—they roll the potatoes down the chute and into the bins to keep for the winter in the cool earthy air.

The kitchen smells sharp with the scent of green tomato chow, and jars are lined up on the end of the table. A pot on the wood stove bubbles richly. We wash our hands at the tap and then sit at the table to say grace. It's a delicious stew of beef with potatoes and carrots and turnip, for the noontime dinner is the main meal of the day.

Back at the potato field, the afternoon passes slowly, and we get bored and restless. The boys pick up small potatoes, the ones not worth keeping, and when the other isn't looking, throw them at each other fast and hard like little bullets. Bernadette and I take frequent breaks to drink from the brook, and splash about in the water, getting leaves and twigs from the overhanging trees caught in our hair.

As we work the soil dribbles into my sneakers, and I slip them off and tuck them into the box of the wagon, close to the front where they won't get lost. The damp soil clings to my old jeans and t-shirt, and leaves muddy trails across my face when I brush a stray hair from my cheek.

By the time the afternoon starts to cool we are bringing home the last load. Tomorrow Papa will let the cows into the field to eat their fill of the tops and the broken ones. We climb into the wagon and the boys head off on a shortcut through the fields and across the river. Papa clicks his tongue at the horses and they start, hardly needing to be guided. Bernadette and I perch on top of the piled potatoes on the back, our muddy bare feet swinging over the end of the boards.

As we drive over the pavement toward our lane, a car pulls up behind us. It's long and white with lots of chrome and tinted glass. Papa clicks again and tugs Buster's rein, pulling over to let the car pass, but instead the car stops and a man jumps out. He wears a very white shirt and charcoal-grey pants, and he's thick in the middle and hunched at the shoulders like someone who has spent a lot of time behind a desk. He speaks to Father in a friendly way, "Do you live near here?"

"I do." Nodding toward our white house visible amid the red out-buildings and green fields.

"Are these your horses?"

A Wagon Load

"They are." Shaking the right rein over the haunches of the lighter horse, "This is Buster," and the left over the darker, "and Ben."

"They're strong-looking horses. And these are your children?"

"Indeed they are."

"Can I take your picture?"

"You can."

The man's voice is one of the nasal American voices we hear from the tourists with New York plates. He runs back to the car and digs out a large impressive camera, black with chrome fittings and a long lens, with which he takes many photos. First of my father on the wagon with the reins in his hand and the fine team of horses, then one from across the road that shows the horses and the wagon, him driving and us sitting on the back of the load, and the cattle grazing in the field beyond. Then he takes one of Papa standing with the team, his hand on Ben's bridle, shoulders back and looking very proud, our house visible beyond the pasture and looking small against the solid bulk of the barn. Then there are three or four of me and Bernadette sitting at the end of the wagon with our bare feet dangling over the edge, mud up to the knees, mud on our old work clothes, mud smeared across our faces, and our hair tangled with leaves from our play among the trees.

Back home with the load, Bernadette and I come inside while Father and the boys send the potatoes down the wooden chute into their bin in the basement, then park the wagon and unhitch the horses. They lead them to the gate of the pasture and let them loose to graze. Mother meets us in the porch with clean clothes, and while we strip off our dirty things in the porch and hop into clean ones, we chatter about the man, pleased at having our pictures taken. Mother glances up, "Oh really?"

When Papa comes with the boys, he sits for tea. Mother brings a plate of biscuits so hot from the oven that they steam when you break them open and the butter melts into liquid pools that drip down the sides and onto your fingers. We are occupied with scooping jam on top and catching the drips when it melts and runs together with the butter. Papa pours the hot tea into his saucer and raises it to his lips.

Once everyone has been fed Mother speaks. "What's this about a tourist taking pictures?"

"Och, it was only a man from the States in a fancy car, and he took pictures."

"Of you and the children?"

"Of the horses, with myself, and the children. He gave me this for our trouble"—pulling an American bill from his shirt pocket. It is a lot of money to us, a welcome addition to the family finances.

"Of the children with dirty faces and no shoes, sitting in the wagon like they were backward. He was making a fool of you. Taking pictures to show back home how we're such hillbillies."

And with one quick movement she sweeps the bill from his hand, opens the lid of the stove and drops it in the embers. A small flare, and it's gone in an instant. The stove lid bangs down.

Bernadette and I sit open-mouthed. We've never seen money wasted before, and we rarely saw our mother cross. It was the first time I consider that perhaps not everyone envies our possession of Buster and Ben, the cattle our father was so proud of, a basement full of potatoes, the sturdy wagon, and the pastures and hayfields and the fertile garden field we work so hard in. I am not sure what is happening, but I know it has to do with the people from New York, and the fancy car.

We put our heads down and play with our food a little, waiting for something more to be said, but nothing is, and after a bit Alex Joe speaks quietly. "The fence in the grain field looks bad, Papa, we'll have to be fixing it in the spring, or the Charolais cow will be getting out."

Ruth Morris Schneider

Behind the Glass

I TURNED TWENTY-SIX IN 1963. I was searching for the centre, for the core of things, attempting to find a point from which I could define myself. That may be why I climbed. Maybe I wanted to yield to nature, to develop a relationship with her, to put myself at the mercy of the elements in order to glean from them a kind of knowledge not available to the casual observer. I wanted to be John Muir in his tree, and an expedition to the Chugach Mountains in Alaska gave me an opportunity to go further into the heart of things than I had ever gone before.

My husband and I had been living in an eastern industrial centre where Aaron was an engineer and I taught language and literature at a small college. We spent every weekend driving to rock-climbing areas. We would leave as early as possible Friday evening and arrive home in time for work Monday morning.

We spent summers in the Rockies, the Kootenays, the Selkirks, or further south in the Tetons or Wind Rivers of Wyoming. That year Dick, a climbing acquaintance who had contacts in Anchorage, suggested climbing Mt. Marcus Baker in Alaska. The mountain had been climbed once before, in 1938, the year of my birth. Dick suggested an expedition to climb a new route beginning on the glacier below the mountain, and he said that the mountaineering club in Anchorage had at least one person from their group who wanted to join such an expedition if it came about. The prospect was exciting.

The three of us left home the second week in June and headed west on the Trans-Canada. Ontario, Manitoba, Saskatchewan, we ticked off the provinces like minutes in an hour glass, passing through Grand Prairie at two o'clock in the morning when nothing moved on the streets and the land stretched out before and after the city like flat breads put out by a housewife to cool. At Dawson Creek we bought plastic covers for the headlights to protect them from flying gravel on the still unpaved Alaska Highway. In Whitehorse we bought steak in the supermarket and cooked it that night over a fire at the edge of the road. We marveled at the high prices of commodities and at the eternity of black spruce that surrounded us. The road was a dusty rope tying Whitehorse to the cities ahead.

We battled mosquitoes even larger than those we had encountered in the back country of British Columbia, and we avoided the campgrounds with their overflowing outhouses and garbage cans surrounded by flies, preferring instead the occasional gravel pit where we pitched tents in the lee of the car. There was little sleep, however, as the late spring sun glowed nightly through the yellow tents.

Our fourth day on the Highway brought us to Anchorage. Our dispositions were frayed by dust, insects and exhaustion, and Anchorage was a disappointment. The city was a frontier town afflicted by cancerous suburban growth. Three months earlier, on Good Friday, there had been an earthquake the results of which could be seen in the rubble along the main street and in the houses tipped precariously off mud cliffs outside the centre of town. And although the offshore volcanic peaks jutted cleanly skyward out of the ocean, the interior Chugach Range shed rotten rock off crumbling peaks. I wanted to head south, to British Columbia and the clean blue granite of the Bugaboos.

But that night I changed my mind. We went to the monthly meeting of the mountain club and I met the climber who wanted to join us. My hopes for a good expedition were revived on two counts: the climber had a lot of experience in the Alaska mountains and she, Ingrid, was a woman.

Two days later we did an air reconnaissance of the Marcus Baker Glacier. "Hey, look at that," the pilot shouted as we flew slowly over the river of ice that would be our route in two days.

On the ridge to our left and slightly ahead moved a large blond grizzly, his coat golden in the late afternoon sun. The pilot tipped us wingward and swung down, expecting to see the grizzly run when the plane drew near. Instead the bear flung back his head, mouth open, and reared onto his hind legs pawing the air and screaming his outrage at the plane, a gigantic insect entering his domain.

"He knows whose country this is," the pilot called back.

A chill ran up my spine.

We could see the glacier stretching from a winding green river at its tongue up to Marcus Baker and Mt. Good, with crevasses giving way to solid snow two-thirds of the way up. The earthquake had shaken everything loose. Ice blocks the size of houses had slid down the sides of cirques pushing soft snow before them. There appeared to be a way through the maze, but at one point the crevasses were so thick we would have to forego the ice and clamber over the moraine, at least a three-hour climb. We figured if we were flown into the Grasshopper landing strip at the bottom of the glacier, the route would take four days then one day more for the climb up Marcus Baker. We would allow six days, and if we had extra time we would climb Mt. Good.

Ingrid needed to make arrangements for the care of her two young children, and we needed to recuperate from our long drive, so we didn't leave Anchorage until the last week in June. Although it was summer, it was a cold day when we began our trek. I remember the wind in my face and the edges of my balaclava freezing against my cheeks when I stood beside the landing strip and watched the plane disappear back towards the city. But our spirits were high as we took a first step on the hitherto untraveled glacier.

It rained later that day, but even then it was beautiful. Rivers of slush poured down the glacier, tumbled into moulins and were whisked down to the very heart of the ice, flowing silently through realms of soft light to the tongue of the glacier, the melting source of the river below. The sun came out and we gazed down one of the moulins, a blue whirlpool moving faster than my eye could follow.

LOCAL HERO

I pictured a person pulled down in those waters, a sub-glacial Alice exploring crystal rabbit holes.

The second day we got higher and light rain turned to snow and then diminished by the day-night evening, when the sun at midnight sat on the horizon for an instant's rest before climbing laboriously back into the sky. The yellow tent heightened the daylight illusion, and our eyes stared at the light, waiting for morning.

That day the sun turned snow into a desert, burning our eyes and skin when we removed parkas that had become too warm. We roped up and moved slowly over crevasse fields, ice axes ready for a sudden arrest, rigging ladders over cracks we couldn't circumvent.

When the glacier turned and dropped into a convexity bristling with falling towers of ice, we worked our way over to the moraine to avoid the seracs. There, glassy ice turned to rotten rock and mud where every ounce in my heavy pack made itself known. With pack straps cutting my shoulders, my back sweating, wet boots rubbing broken blisters on my raw heels, I felt my energy dissipate and began to think that making a second ascent of a peak climbed twenty-five years earlier was the height of stupidity. But when we stood at the top of the moraine the glacier stretched out above and below us, gleaming its invitation to go on to the top and into the wonderland seen only by bush pilots from their planes.

The third day was glorious. At seven thousand feet we had reached the smooth light snow above the open crevasse field and could walk easily on snowshoes. This was a marshmallow-cream world with every rise in the terrain covered with white topping. We improvised headgear from white cloth foodbags and moved like Bedouins against the sun, laughing at our shadows. Our energies revived, we dropped our packs and capered on the landscape, turning somersaults in the snow.

We made our base camp on the fourth day at the bottom of a cirque that dropped like an epaulet from the shoulder of Marcus Baker. The sun was temporarily blocked by the west wall of the cirque and a fine white mist settled in, muffling our voices and making us aware, for the first time, of our isolation.

Our spirits dropped as suddenly as they had risen and our earlier exhaustion returned along with an unnamed anxiety. We did our camping chores either silently or with sharp words. We quarreled about the cooking and the melting of snow for water, and we cast anxious glances at the mountain as it became gradually obscured in the mist.

White clouds moved in that night and the rock candy landscape beneath us disappeared, leaving only the jaw of the cirque, overhung by a broken cornice from which large chunks of snow and ice had fallen like rotten teeth. We slept little and the following morning tempers were short. We argued about the weather, some saying the clouds would lift as the morning wore on, others that we had allowed an extra day, why not take it? Yet if it were possible to climb Marcus Baker today we could make a first ascent on Mt. Good tomorrow, in this way gaining two peaks for our expedition.

And we argued about the route on the now nearly invisible Marcus Baker: whether to hike around the side of the cirque, staying well behind the cornice, and then go up the shoulder, or to go directly up the headwall of the cirque. While the latter would be quicker, the former would be safer. For the first time the tent was too small to hold our four personalities and perhaps this was why we decided not only to climb, but to go directly up the headwall.

We also left the snowshoes behind, feeling they would be a hindrance once the climbing became steep, and we started out unroped. The soft snow gave way beneath our feet and we sank in further each time we moved. My own anger with the day, the conditions, and my comrades grew with every step.

When it was my turn to break trail I resentfully pushed ahead, glancing back at the flags we'd placed behind us. It had begun to snow, and those tiny flags, made one evening by the fireplace out of tomato stakes and red cloth, would become our way back to camp if the white-out became complete. They grew out of the snow like poppies.

Fueled by anger I pushed ahead, sank in, and pushed again.

Beside me was the dim outline of an ice block dropped from the cornice; beyond it, I thought, the walking would become easier. I couldn't tell how far we had come up the wall of the cirque as the blending of snow and sky made steepness a matter of feel and guess. I had heard stories of climbers thinking they were on level ground when actually they were climbing. Certainly I was winded, but that might have been from moving in deep snow, or from anger.

The next step, however, brought the snow to my waist.

"It won't go," I thought, and I turned to those behind me.

They were tending to the flagging, and I waited for someone to look forward again, having no breath to call but an eternity to wait. I stood with the snow encircling my waist and stretching out as far as I could see. It was as though I were wearing the earth like a crinoline and the figures moving in the mist danced on my skirt.

Suddenly the snow settled as if it would adjust my weight more equitably and I sank in to my armpits.

I called, too softly, to the nearest figure.

Then my throat closed as I realized my legs hung free. I had sunk into snow covering the bergschrund, the predictable crevasse where the ice of a glacier breaks away from the mountain, something we would have known we were near had we been able to see how high we'd come.

With a jolt, time started up again as I broke through the crust. Snow and ice flew in chunks around me as I fell; wildly awake, I felt both the speed of the fall and fear of being buried in snow. My back brushed the vertical wall down which I sped, slowing my movement, but then the wall dropped away and the rate of my descent increased. I was in an elevator shaft leading into the bowels of the glacier to be deposited and frozen into the slow moving ice for a millennium until I would be spat off the glacier's tongue, a time capsule recording a human's attempt to play with nature.

A sudden shock of pain shot through my left leg and side. My climbing rope, coiled uselessly around my shoulder, disappeared below me, along with my ice axe, hat and goggles as I was flipped upside down. Snow powdered my body and face and combed through my hair. In the silence that followed, I heard myself scream.

My left leg, caught on a thin ice fence coming out from the side of the bergschrund, was wedged in by a chunk of hard snow that had broken off from its lip. I hung upside down like a broken doll. Beneath me the ice fell away, turning from sapphire to azure to black. I couldn't see the bottom. Sixty feet above me I saw Aaron's stricken face outlined by the blue of his parka. He yelled at me not to move and he threw down a rope which I tied around my waist.

A second rope was thrown with a loop for me to stand in on my right leg and be hauled up. A sling to slip under my arms was attached further up, and, once secured, I was able to release my injured left leg from the ice that wedged it in. Aaron and Dick hauled me out as I pulled hand over hand on the rope I'd tied around my waist while Ingrid took up the slack. The ropes cut through the soft edge of the bergschrund making the last few feet a snow bath through which I emerged like a newborn snow-baby.

My left leg was useless. I was helped back down the line of flags to the tent which was then collapsed and folded into a primitive sled on which I was dragged several miles back down to 7500 feet and the top of the open crevasse field where we set up camp.

Real fear didn't come until that night. Then, while others slept in exhaustion, I lay awake hearing the voices of the bergschrund laughing, and I realized for the first time in my twenty-six years that I could die.

The following day was clear. Our bush pilot flew in to see how the climb was going and responded to our signal to call the Rescue Communications Center, dropping low and cutting his engine to shout "The RCC is coming!"

In the rescue helicopter, all the details of our four-day trek blended into a twenty-minute blur as we flew back to the city opening like a wound on the shore. I watched cars racing down the main street and ladies window shopping on their lunch hour, and weariness pressed in on me like the blue ice.

After that summer we bought a house and a few acres in New

England. We continued going west to the mountains whenever we traveled. We traversed ranges and climbed peaks, but I knew that having gone to the edge I had found my centre.

Larry Gibbons

To Catch a Coin

WHY THE HELL IS THIS ANXIETY SHIT WORSE when I drive through Haunted River Reserve? I mean, I can barely drag my foot up on the brake pedal to get the damn car to slow down. And then, where do I end up parking? In front of the reserve cemetery. The grave markers creeping me out with a sort of stifling guilt. I'm totally frozen behind the steering wheel, like a bird who's bashed his noggin into a window. Sitting here feeling catatonic.

I'm shocked out of this immobility by an Aboriginal woman, who taps on my window, then opens the door. She helps me out of the car. Her face is kind and she looks at me like I'm the only person in the world besides her. She invites me to her home.

I follow her to her house like an SPCA rescued dog, where she offers me a cup of boiling hot tea and a biscuit. She talks to me and calms me enough that I can get back into my car and journey on.

These screwed-up emotions began about a month ago. I'd been returning from an auction near Shubenacadie, where I'd purchased an old school desk and a few other odds and ends.

I'd decided, for no particular reason, to pull over by the "Welcome to Haunted River Reserve" sign. I scrambled down through the litter and animal crap until I was under the Haunted River bridge. The dark water was bubbling and swirling something terrible and I remember how loudly it hissed as it headed towards the ocean.

I'd barely planted my ass down alongside of the river, when I'd felt a frightening urge to jump into the water. And I'd heard voices. I was clueless as to what they were saying. I know they weren't speaking English. Ever since I stopped at the river, I've had a foreboding seep like a dripping tap into the rest of my emotional safety zones.

Today is Good Friday, and I'm heading to a place not far from Port Hawkesbury. Yesterday, a woman phoned and told me she had a photo for me to see. She'd said the photo had a feeling about it.

I've been an antique dealer for thirty years. I know the effect antiques can have. They shed feelings like old skin and can change the mood in my shop. Some, I can't wait to sell and get them the hell out of my place.

I locate her blue, wooden, two-storey house. A cardboard sign is nailed to a crooked porch post, warning people to watch their step. The concrete slabs are loose and wobbly.

The old woman, wearing bright red slippers, leads me up a narrow flight of stairs. Photos and pictures peer down from the silver wallpaper. Another four steps lead to an attic room. The door is open. She flicks on the light which highlights an ancient, bronze-trimmed chest parked in the middle of the stuffy room.

She removes a brown paper bag from the chest. Pulls out a photo and hands it to me and, cripes, I'm afraid to look at it. I feel once again the hypnotic and suffocating charm of the Haunted River licking at my feet.

I have to sit on an antique stool. I struggle to say, "The photo smells smoky."

"It's amazing you can still smell the smoke."

"Why are you thinking of giving this picture to me?" I hold the photo like it's a limp rabbit I've removed from a snare.

"When I was at your store, you told me about your emotional reactions when you passed through the reserve. The story touched me and when I thought about giving away the photo, it was your name that jumped into my mind."

I turn the photo over and look at it. I hold it with both hands. It's an eight-by-ten, black-and-white picture of an Aboriginal boy. He's stuffing a spoonful of food into his mouth and is gazing at something in front of and above him. His eyes are like a rabbit's, nervously watching a flying murder of zealous crows. I look away when I see the sad cereal-bowl haircut. Feelings clamp onto my screwed-up mind like a disturbed snapping turtle. Maybe indignation. My heart flips a bird in my chest.

I hand the photo back to the woman.

"Where did you get that photo?"

"Come on, I'll make you a cup of tea. I can tell I'm giving the photo to the right person."

"Or the wrong person," I say. "Could I have a glass of water too?"

I want to take one of my tranquilizer pills. I'm going to have to renew the prescription.

The woman told me, "Quite a few years ago, I was returning from Halifax, with my now deceased husband. We were approaching Shubenacadie when we spotted the smoke and flames. It was a ferocious fire with embers and chunks of bricks shooting up into the dusky sky, like popcorn in a microwave. We could feel the heat when we pulled over to watch.

"A crowd of Aboriginals were in the field cheering. When a wall of the abandoned school collapsed, I thought they were going to shout the sky down on top of us.

"The strange part happened when we arrived home. As we were unloading the car, I found that brown bag with the photo in it. I've got no idea where the photo came from."

"So this photo is of a boy from the Shubenacadie Residential School?"

"That's my theory."

"Why don't you give it to an Aboriginal person or to a museum?"

"Maybe because the photo had such an effect on me and I didn't want to part with it until I understood what I was feeling. Like, was there a reason why I found it? I think you're the reason.

"And you know what I thought when I first looked at the

photo?" the woman said. "I thought it might be a revelation from Jesus Christ. Strange thought, and I have no idea why I would think that."

I'm about ten K from Haunted River Reserve. I see a short fella, maybe in his fifties or sixties, hitchhiking. He's wearing thick baggy pants and a construction glow-in-the-dark vest. I pick him up.

"Where you heading?" I ask.

"Haunted River Reserve."

Soon as he says that, my digestive plumbing breaks into a brisk canter.

We don't talk much until we pass a black pipe which protrudes out from the bottom of a mountain. It spews spring water onto the side of the road.

The hitchhiker points at the pipe and says, "I carved my father's name into that birch tree by the pipe. That's where I found one of his coins. In a puddle. Every place I find his coin I carve his name."

"Why do you do that?"

"I'm making my father his own Stations of the Cross. That pipe was number three coin. You know where number two was? In the toilet bowl after I had a crap."

He laughs. I laugh too, because it's damn funny. Whacko, but funny.

"My father carved. He was the best and I'm not shitting you. He started carving animals out of pieces of firewood when he was at the residential school. My father said the place was worse than jail."

The hitchhiker pulls a fat leather bag out of his pants pocket. He unzips it, leans over and lets me look into the pouch. I smell sweet grass and tobacco.

"Thirteen coins in there. All quarters. My father made the bag out of a preacher's leather Bible cover."

I'm thinking, hell, people are always dropping their god damn coins.

"How do you know they're from your father?"

"Because all the coins have 1945 on them. That's the year he was forced to go to the residential school."

The hitchhiker's eyes are darting around like a bug in a jug and his breath smells like fermented mouthwash.

I take out a quarter. Nineteen-forty-five. God damn, but if they're not all nineteen-forty-five quarters.

I wonder, "Is this guy jerking me around?" Because he's always wearing this muted offshoot of a Cheshire grin on his bristly mug.

And all this time, the hitchhiker is poke peeking at the brown paper bag lying on the armrest. Then my car hits another damn pothole and part of the photo jerks out of the bag.

"Mind if I look at that picture?"

I hand him the photo.

"Holy shit. That's my father. Last I saw this picture, it was hanging on the wall in my mother's insane asylum room. My mother said it disappeared off her wall on Good Friday. We thought our mother might have destroyed it. She never forgave my father for jumping off the bridge. Where'd you get the photo?"

"An old woman gave it to me."

"Aboriginal?"

"Nope. White."

I begin thinking, maybe the reason I got the photo was so I could re-unite it with the family. Maybe this is what all my free-floating anxiety is about. It's a premonition.

The hitchhiker partially unzips his jacket and pulls out a small carving hanging around his neck.

"My father carved this. It's a carving of the salmon an eagle dropped on his head when he was trout fishing on the lake."

The wee salmon looks so life-like I'm expecting it to open and close its mouth and begin breathing.

"It's really detailed," I say.

"My father always carved his initials into his carvings. See? 'JI.' His name was Johnny Isadore. Ever since I started getting coins from my father, I've never missed a Good Friday Procession. I almost missed today's. You must have been chosen to pick me up. You're like a disciple."

"I'm only on the road because of this photo." I wiggle my toes to make sure I can.

"My father carved a squirrel when he was at the school. When a mean nun threw him into the dungeon, his squirrel carving came to life. Even brought him food. Good food from the priest's cupboard. That's one of my father's miracles."

He reaches into his pocket and pulls out a shiny, mean-looking knife. Which has the effect of stopping any of my lingering catatonia in its tracks.

"This is what I carve with. It's my father's knife."

I'm glad the hitchhiker puts the knife back into his pocket.

I think I better ask this fella if he wants the photo because we're approaching the "Welcome to Haunted River Reserve" sign.

"I carved my father's name in the signpost there. The right back post. That's my father's tenth Station of the Cross. I spend lots of time sitting by the river listening to my father. That's how I know number fourteen is the final holy coin. One more coin and I'm going to stop walking in the Good Friday Processions. That's the number he told me."

"Your father jumps off a fuck'n bridge to give you coins?" My toes are numbing up and passing off to my ankles.

"He wanted to be like Christ and die for all the survivors from the school."

"Oh, come on," I think. But I say: "How is your father jumping into the river and killing himself, helping?"

"You don't have to believe me. You look like a guy who has a lot of cynic running in your blood, but people can, when they sleep, dream of going to all the places where I found his coins and carved his initials. I find the fourteenth coin and I'm going to be with him and the Blessed Mother. He says he'll be waiting for me on Good Friday."

This has got to be a trainload of total bullshit, surely. And damn it, when we get around the corner, I see the goddamn procession unwinding its way from the little white church and filling up the highway. The priest's white robe waving like a surrender flag. The thick clouds are choking off the sun and it's as dark as I'd expect it to be on Good Friday.

And a damn police car blocks the road. I'm going to have to sit here until the procession has cleared the road. I'm nailed to the highway.

"Where does the procession turn off?" I ask.

"Just after the bridge. It goes around the reserve."

The damn bridge is about a half kilometre away.

I say, "I want you to have the photo." Actually, I want to grab him and say, "Take it for shit sake."

"Listen Bud," he says, "it's your picture. You must have it for a reason. Just like you picked me up for a reason. You're part of my father's Good Friday miracle story."

His Cheshire grin morphs into a harsh phlegmy chuckle while the jerk-off in my brain tightens the vise on my head.

Maybe I should pitch the damn photo out the window. For another right person to find it. Right person to right person.

"Why don't you keep collecting the coins, so you can carve your father's name more places?"

"I'll carve one more station, once I get the last coin. No orders from the Bible or nuns. My father chose his day just like Jesus chose his. Maybe Jesus didn't have it so hard."

"Why's that?"

"You okay? You look shaky and kind of pale."

"I really want to know why you said what you said."

"'Cause Jesus was in control. Jumping in on Good Friday was my father making it his time. The nuns only talked about the stories in their book. My father made a story."

No wonder his mother's in a loony bin.

"Thanks for the ride."

"Here, take the photo," I shout. "He's your father."

"It's yours," he says. "It's in your eyes. You're part of the Good Friday story."

Then the hitchhiker jumps out of my car. And this is no word of a lie. He gets a few feet up the road when I see him stop and pick something up. I'm sure it's a coin because I watch him inspect it, then pull out his Bible-covered bag and deposit it into the pouch.

My breathing is thick and anxious as I watch the procession pass the old coffin factory and slowly wind its way to the Haunted River Bridge.

I hear the guy behind me, whose window is open, swearing at the procession because he's in a hurry for some meeting. Maybe his own Good Friday service. But he's in no more of a hurry than I am.

What surprises me is feeling my anxiety ease up after the hitchhiker left my car. And I'm suspecting it's because of my peculiar feeling—kind of like leaving a cramped cage and entering a massive open amphitheatre.

All the way to Sydney I ask myself, will the hitchhiker jump? Could I have said something to make him look at things differently? What am I going to do with the damn photo?

I feel like a cornered rabbit with the photo of the young boy resting on the seat beside me. Dangerous, prophetic and maybe owning the right to being goddamn vindictive.

First thing I do when I get to my antique shop, except for making a strong rum and coke, is go through my drawers and cupboards. Where, after some scratching around, I find the rabbit carving. Perfect in every detail, and on its underbelly, I find those goddamn initials, "JI."

I pour another drink and then put the carving along with the photo on the desk I'd bought at the auction. Strangely, I think of the Trinity when I look at them.

When I search the desk, I already know what I will find. And there it is. Carved into the rim of the desktop. "JI."

I plunk myself back down on the wicker chair. Hear a coin fall to the floor. Clink and jiggle as it rolls to a stop. I hesitate before picking it up.

Jigs Gardner

Owly Bob

I WAS SITTING WITH THE STOREKEEPER on a bench in his backyard, drinking beer. I had finished mowing his field, the horses were standing in the shade switching their tails at flies, and it was time for a rest and a chat.

"Do you know a guy I often see along the road fishing? Big guy, tall, barrel chest. Somebody said he was called Two-gun."

"Oh, yes. Two-gun."

"Why's he called that?"

"Big mouth, always spouting off. Steer clear of him—he's owly."

"Owly? What's that supposed to mean?"

"You don't know? I thought Americans knew everything."

"Cut it out. What does 'owly' mean?"

"Hang around Two-gun and you'll find out."

That was all I learned from the storekeeper—then.

I had seen him fishing at the Cove on my way to town, and also on the road to the sawmill a couple of times, and the last time I had stopped the horses and asked how the fish were biting.

His only answer, with a sweeping gesture, was, "I'm enjoyin' the beauties of Mother Nature!"

I laughed and drove on.

On the way home from the storekeeper's that day, hauling the mowing machine on the wagon, I saw him at the Cove. I stopped, asked about the fishing again, but his attention was fixed on an eagle that had just landed on a tree across the Cove. Pointing to it he proclaimed, "The monarch of the skies!" An eccentric of some sort, I thought, as I started the horses; maybe that's what "owly" means.

The following Friday evening, just after dark, a car drove in. I turned on the porch light and opened the screen door. It was Two-gun, wearing a jacket and tie, all spruced up, a formidable figure, and behind him was a wizened old man wearing a windbreaker and a railroad man's cap. Two-gun took the kitchen by storm. "Hello! The House!" he bellowed. "God bless all here!" He shook my hand, shook Jo Ann's, and sat at the head of the table. "My friend, Richard Matheson," waving at the little old man at the end of the table.

When anyone enters your house in Cape Breton you immediately pour him a cup of tea and offer him a slice of bannoch if you have it, otherwise cookies will do. I went to the stove for the tea while Jo Ann got out the cookies.

"I'm Bob Morrison, down from Sydney to pursue the finny tribe and have some fun."

I knew what "fun" meant in Cape Breton spoken with relish like that: drink and plenty of it. When we first came I had innocently let it be known that I made beer and wine, and we had been plagued by alcoholics, so now I never offered anyone a drink. But they seemed content with tea and cookies; in fact, Bob cleaned the plate and asked for more.

The conversation was largely about people on the peninsula, mostly scandalous rumours, the usual countryside talk. Bob dominated the conversation, but Richard maintained a persistent running argument about someone who'd promised to get a bottle but hadn't, while Bob insisted that he hadn't *promised* a bottle, but said he'd *try* to get one. We did learn that Bob worked at the steel mill in Sydney, had a wife and two children, but spent most weekends on the peninsula, fishing and hunting, but from the way they spoke of their endeavours, mostly stories about missed opportunities and disasters, I gathered that these things were really only excuses for jolly weekends of general carrying on. This was an old story on the peninsula: bums from Sydney came to the area because it was wilder, sparsely populated with the Canadian equivalent of hillbillies, and you almost never saw a Mountie there. I had encountered men like that over the years—they were always curious about our beautiful farm in the depths of the empty Backlands—and I kept out of their way, but Bob seemed a happy-go-lucky version and they didn't stay long, perhaps an hour, and we enjoyed the visit. We had friends here and there, but they were mostly farmers and woodsmen, not people who would come by for an evening visit.

Thus began the first year of our friendship with Bob Morrison, a year of Friday evening visits of an hour or so, maybe twice a month, and every visit was more or less like that first one, with two exceptions. Once they brought along a woman, Margaret MacNeil, in whose house Richard had a room. She was remarkable for her aloof reticence—she hardly said ten words—and her appearance. She looked amazingly like an aged Dragon Lady from the old Terry and the Pirates comic strip with her dyed black hair, her long cigarette holder, her heavily powdered face and vivid lipstick.

Parenthetically, I had a funny conversation with a friend when we were dismantling a barn some years later. Margaret MacNeil had just died and my friend noted it. I said the only time I had seen her she looked like a black widow spider, to which he replied that she was "a handsome woman in her day," and I answered, "We were all good looking in our day." After a long moment he said, smugly I thought, "Some of us were, and some of us weren't."

The other exception was the night he came alone with a schoolbook he had found in a derelict shack, an anthology of the poetry taught in schools a century ago. Bob wanted me to read some aloud because, he said, "You got the education to bring out the poetry." I turned the pages, looking for the sort of poem I thought he'd like, lots of resonance and spirit: "The Battle Hymn of the Republic," Tennyson's "Blow, Bugle, Blow," a couple of ballads, "Invictus," Blake's "Tiger," "O Captain, My Captain." I put all my expression into it, and he seemed to love it.

Our half-mile lane was blocked by snow, so we didn't see Bob in the winter. The next summer he turned up, along with Richard, on a Friday in April, and we didn't see him again until the beginning of June, on a Saturday afternoon, and ever afterward we saw him only on Saturday afternoons.

I hadn't thought about it, but on Fridays he was fresh from Sydney, all dressed up, and dissipation had not yet taken its toll. Now all the Friday clothes were gone, replaced by shabby country clothes, and Bob himself, unshaven with bloodshot eyes, was a different man. He'd drive in, alone or with Richard or someone else, and stay for lunch, and it was obvious from his raucousness that he'd been drinking though I wouldn't say he was drunk. It was obviously a demotion, a diminution in respect, when we descended from Fridays to Saturdays.

Bob drove in one day with a new pal I had never seen before, horribly obsequious, who kept calling me "Sir." I was working in the shop filing a six-foot crosscut saw while Bob prowled around the shop and the other guy asked questions about how the forge worked. Finally Bob asked for a bottle of my wine. I told him we served it only at meals. He muttered something and kicked about the forge. I went on filing.

Bob said in a surly tone, "You think you're hot stuff, don't you?" Holding the file poised over the saw, I looked straight at him and said quietly, "Is this how you got the reputation of being owly?" By then, I had figured out its meaning. He couldn't look at me. "Ah, to hell with you," he weakly grumbled as he slouched out. Mr. Obsequious was distressed. "Oh, sir, don't mind Bobby, sir. That's the drink talkin', you know Bobby's got a heart of gold, sir."

I thought that was the end, but a week later I was asleep on the couch in the living room with a mild case of flu, when the blanket was pulled away from my head and I woke to behold Bob, his dirty pants held up by baling twine, no shirt, looking as if he'd just crawled out of a coal mine. "John, gimmie some wine."

"Oh Bob, I'm sick, go 'way."

Jo Ann was eighty yards away at the barn, but she recognized

Bob's car and headed for the house. We were still arguing when she walked in and ordered Bob out. She was standing by the door, and as he went out he deliberately brushed hard against her.

We didn't see him again for three years. We were running a hostel then, and sometimes hitchhikers would get a ride in. It was after supper, guests were sitting out on the porch, and I was washing the dishes. A vehicle drove in with a hosteller, and Jo Ann went to sign her in. The driver opened the screen door. It was Bob, utterly changed. The barrel chest had dropped to his waist, and he looked old and haggard. "Hi, Bob. What's new?"

"I retired, John." There was a pause, and then he said, very lugubriously, "I'm dyin', John."

"What? What is it?"

"I'm dyin' o' loneliness," again very plaintively.

I laughed so hard I dropped a plate. "See what you done?" he said happily. By the time I had picked up the plate, he was gone, pleased with his small success, no doubt, but wary of pushing his luck. That was our last encounter. Over the next few years I heard about him occasionally. Tolerated when he was in his prime, now he found it very difficult to find a berth. Finally he tried to move in on some of the crabby old pensioners, squatting in shacks along the back roads, living from one glorious drunk each month to the next, but he got short shrift there. Last I heard he was living in his car, parking in the overgrown lanes to heat coffee over a campfire.

Once again I had mown the storekeeper's field, and once again I was sitting on a bench drinking beer with the storekeeper as the horses stood in the shade, switching their tails at flies.

"I wonder what happened to Two-gun last winter. Last I heard he was living in his car. He couldn't've been doing that in the winter."

"He stayed here."

"WHAT?"

"Oh, not in my house. There's a little building not much

more than a shack, out behind the barn. We used it when we were rebuilding after the fire."

"You told me to stay away from him, told me he was owly."

"Well, I didn't have him here in the house. His wife kicked him out, you know. And no one would put up with him.... You've got two cabins empty all winter, you could've put him up."

"Like hell!"

The storekeeper smiled. "You entertained him in your house, you told me how he liked poetry, how funny he was."

"That's before I knew how owly he was."

"Oh yes, he was owly all right—but he was a human being."

"You amaze me."

"The feeling is mutual."

We laughed.

A year or so later I got an envelope in the mail from the storekeeper. Inside was a clipping from the obituary column of the Sydney paper with notice of Robert Morrison's death. He was survived by his wife and two children. Also in the envelope was one of the storekeeper's billheads, and on it he had written "Now let God judge him."

I folded the billhead and stuck it in my wallet. And there it remains, its worn creases showing where it has been unfolded and folded again and again.

Teresa O'Brien

To Country Living

WE HAD BEEN LIVING IN THE TOWN for almost twenty years when the piece of land out by the sea came up for sale. Luke had always wanted a place in the country and it had become something of a habit, driving out that way on those Sunday afternoons when we didn't know what else to do with ourselves. Luke imagined Canada geese filling the inlet, places for hides. I saw myself in a lean kayak slipping along reedy shores. Blue herons, beaver dams. We had both thought of some livestock, a few chickens. But when I thought about it later, I realized that it was Luke who was truly in love with the land. And while I had agreed with him over the years that it would be great to have a view, a vista as I called it, I know now that I really did not want to live in the country. Nor did our children.

What? Here, you mean? they said incredulously when asked for their opinion. Eventually, they refused to go out there at all.

That Easter, the land was listed and Luke put in a bid. Paul and Zach were home from university and Luke insisted that we all go out and take a walk over the property. We tramped along in the raw cold, through the crackling branches and over the soggy ground, the boys complaining bitterly about getting soaked and ruining their sneakers. There was a clearing, the site of an old house or barn, the brambles grown up about it. As we walked through, the brambles catching our sweaters and trousers, I became increasingly resentful because it seemed to me that when I went for a walk with Luke, we always ended up in bramble. Or bog. Or both.

We were marching along behind him, he cheerful and oblivious, and my seeping anger turned to a sense of dread, that this was about to take place. That I might actually live in this bog and bramble.

LOCAL HERO

Just then, I caught a movement by the edge of the clearing. A coyote had stopped, its head turned towards me. The tawny yellow pelt blended with the dried grasses. The coyote stood for a few more minutes before it loped away into the woods. I felt prickles of sweat despite the cold. I had never worried about coyotes until the last few years when there had been increasingly severe attacks. A child bitten while she played outside her back door, small dogs let out for a late night run mauled to death. A cyclist's leg savaged. And that summer, inexplicably, dreadfully, a young woman attacked and killed.

We should go back, I said, running up to join the others who had also stopped to look at the coyote. Paul said, Yes, we should, Dad. But Luke laughed it off, saying, They're more afraid of us than we are of them and, all excitement, unslung his backpack. The clink of glass on glass. The cold, the miserable grey flatness, the complaining children. The coyote. Luke was pouring dark rum toddies from a thermos and handing them out. I had grown so used to agreeing with Luke that a place in the country would be lovely that, now that the two hundred acres of mostly spruce but with a few good trees and plenty of shoreline had come up for sale, I found myself backed into a corner.

To country living, Luke said, raising his glass. Didn't think you'd be up for champagne on a day like this. He turned around, patently proud of the scene. His family, the land. The hot toddies.

We gamely drank the rum and then, with what Luke called unseemly haste, formed a small tight group and returned to the car.

The last few times I have driven out that way all I have seen is the scrubbiness of the land, the dirt road, the distance. Every time I approached the property, I was on the lookout for coyotes. Once, when Luke and I went snowshoeing, we found a deep hole dug in the snow, full of hare bones and fur and thick yellow markings. I was fascinated. Now, I have come to see this newly bought land as a dense, frightening place.

Yehudi Menuhin is playing Beethoven's *Violin Concerto in D*. It is an old LP, scratched, but I don't mind. I adjust the treble and lower the bass. It is a quiet day in the shop. A good day to do some stocktaking and place orders. I change the LP, carefully dusting the vinyl with anti static, and turn up the volume on the Largo from "Winter." I turn it up further, partly because I love this piece, but also to drown out the Celtic music blaring from the gift shop next door. The big Bose speakers tremble as the music forms a protective shield about me. I float in the music, in the bright frame of my shop with its smell of leather. I would be happy if nobody came in today.

Ours is one of the few remaining independent stores in the town. I'm good with people. I have an eye for style. During my university years I amassed a collection of brightly coloured boots, magenta, lavender, chartreuse. And spent more time in concert halls and churches listening to Bach cantatas and Handel largos than I had in lecture halls or libraries. I never finished my degree. When Luke took over his parents' shoe shop, I was pregnant with Paul. Over the years I have forgotten that time, that move. The settling into a small town.

You're Luke's wife? Charge it to Luke's account? Tell Luke to call me about it.

You've managed to fit in so well, Luke sometimes said. I know it suits him to think that. Sometimes I think that I can't stand the place, that there is no future here, that some places are just destined to become ghost towns once all their resources are gone. The early morning charter flights are filled with the young and the too-old heading out to the tar sands, twelve-hour shifts, ten days straight. The town is a post-industrial war field of lost souls, ruined houses and boarded-up businesses. In December two men were found dead outside a rooming house. Throughout that winter there were ten more deaths. A film crew came from Toronto to do a documentary on the effects of what they called an epidemic of oxycontin use in the town. They talked about the crash of the coal industry, the loss of well-paid jobs and a sense of community. The shots were all taken on dismal, foggy days and in bleak, empty lots and rundown buildings with wires and siding flapping against them in the wind.

Sometimes I see a patrol car squeal into a parking lot or stop by a disused doorway or one of the park benches after a tip-off. I've seen the exchanges, the rolled-down window, the shuffling and quick glances, but I have never called the police.

Luke is more righteous. From the office in the shop we have a clear view of the parking lot at the back of town. I do all the ordering but Luke likes to use the office as a headquarters for the town's community campaigns. I often find him hovering by the window, noting the numbers on license plates. Sometimes he would sit for hours by that window. Watching. Spying. I hate when he does this. It is as if a pall has been cast over the beautiful leather boots and suede shoes. They seem pointless, frivolous even, when he is in the shop.

Leave it, Luke. Our boys are okay, they're out of it now.

What about the other boys, Esther? Andrew? And Jason? And Brad? What about them? What about their parents, going in to find them dead in their beds from overdoses of percs and oxys? What about Jimmy? And my heart is sore when I think of Jimmy.

I love the smell of your food, Jimmy used to say, lingering by the stove as I cooked dinner.

It's curried chicken, Jimmy. Try it.

No, Ma'll have dinner waiting for me.

There was a bit on the news last night, Luke says, about men in Dublin defending their neighbourhood from the drug lords.

The drug lords! You sound like a Hollywood film, Luke. And who, precisely, would they be? Johnny next door? Art? After all, he just bought himself a new Mustang.

There you go again. It's all right to laugh, Esther, he says. I don't know why you always have to take the other side.

There I go again. Not being responsible. Not taking your side. I think but do not say. Why bother? There would just be more bickering, cold passing on the stairs.

He has lost his sense of humour. Not that it was ever brilliant anyway. But now he uses phrases like "take back the streets" and "do our duty" totally without irony. There is about him a complacency, a self-satisfied smugness that is beginning to repel me.

And out in the country the concrete has been poured and there's a skeleton of a house and the temporary road is rutted from the deliveries of building supplies. Luke expects that we will be able to use it at Christmas. It won't be finished but we can cut a tree from the land and maybe spend one or two nights there, he'd said. I have not mentioned this to the boys.

On a bright, cold day a young father comes in looking for pink Crocs for his little girl. The kids all love them, adults too, although I find them particularly nasty on grown-ups. I can't imagine what feet would smell like after a summer day slithering around in that plastic, but they are our best sellers. The child had lost one of hers and even though he should have been looking for snow boots, That's what she wants, the father says. The child's size is not in stock, I tell him, but we can order them. I ask him for his phone number. The father smiles. Sure, he says and follows me into the office.

He stops when he sees the window, Luke at the desk, his index finger on the phone dial. There's a bunch of lads outside, a blue car, windows rolled down, somebody hunkered in the back seat, the boys putting small packages in their pockets. A Rottweiler on a short chain lunges and barks. Luke settles the phone back in its cradle when he sees the man. The father turns to me, his face set. He reaches his hand for the child's, the sleeve on his leather jacket riding up to reveal part of an intricate tattoo, pale blue and green flowers and mermaids and wide-eyed girls.

As I walk home that evening I can hear music from one of the old houses that have been let to students from the university in the nearby city. Students from Saudi Arabia, China, Kuwait, Egypt, Pakistan. Arabic music, rhythmic and intense. And the spices from their cooking fill the air, cumin and coriander and garam masala.

I'm from Luxor, one of the young men told me when I got chatting with him.

Will you go back there? I asked. Litter swirled in a vacant lot and a cold wind blew in off the sea. His name was Kareem. I looked for him again when I was out walking but he was not around.

October stars shine murkily in the town lights. Soon, Luke will be going off for his annual hunting trip with his buddies. He mentioned a few times that it would be nice if I could maybe do a little painting, start getting the country place sorted for Christmas.

On the drive out, I catch a glimpse of a man at a window—unaware of my gaze, vulnerable, exposed. There is something unspeakably sad about him. And then the road, empty and dark, one small faded green house set into the trees, rusty trikes and bikes outside. A few trailers, backyard car repair garages, tires and doors and fenders, overgrown gardens—and then just the blackness and the spruce. Down by the end of the road, two men in hunter's orange haul their cumbersome bodies into their pick-up truck and drive away.

Snow has been falling all afternoon and now the snow and the dark are too thick for me to see beyond the house to the line of trees. I turn on the high beams but the snowflakes are bigger, thicker in the bright light. So I sound the horn a few times and then make a quick dash for the door. There had been several articles in the papers by biologists arguing that people would just have to learn to live with coyotes. Rationally I believed them. But on this night, out here, alone, what had reason to do with anything? Quickly, I unload the radio, the hamper of food and wine.

Beyond the cottage, pressing in from the empty country, the dark trees and shadows and animals of the night. I look out the windows, one by one, but there are no tracks in the snow. Nothing but space and silence all around. The house is cold and barren. Burnt orange, sienna, terracotta paint cards litter the countertop. The basement as well as the upstairs is unfinished. The pine mouldings raw. A bare bulb, a scatter of shavings. I am about to turn the lock on the door when I stop myself. Neither Luke nor I ever bothered to lock our back door in town until we were going to bed. And Luke says it's a lot safer in the country. Cross with myself, I crumple newspaper and light the fire, then I busy myself at the stove with a pot of pasta and some ready-made sauce.

Steam rises from the pot and condenses on the windows. There are no curtains yet or blinds and I recall those people looking vulnerable and conspicuous in their country houses. My flat in the city had been directly at street level. Red futons, Ophelia white walls. A stack of records on a chair. They lived in my room, Gould and Bach and Beethoven. Late night take-outs. Friends on my futons, lovers in my bed. And outside the city full of noise and edge and promise.

I pour a glass of wine and try to settle by the fire that is crackling and sparking with all that kindling but the noise just adds to my unease. I feel stared at, witnessed from an unseen vantage point. I could have asked one of my friends to join me for the evening but something stopped me. I have my cell phone. I could call the boys, but it's a Friday night.

Have to go, Mom, they would say after a few minutes, maybe, maybe not taking time to wonder why I had called as they rush for showers, drinks, sushi. I remember them, running against the wind, wind tears on their faces as Ravel's *Bolero* blared from the car. It was so easy then, when they were young and I could gather them to me.

Luke would be fine here on his own, absolutely fine, and again there is that seeping anger. A log explodes in a shower of sparks and cinders, small charred remnants of newspaper flutter about the room. I stamp the cinders, set the screen before the fire. There is a sudden cold draught and I am turning towards the door when my arms are pinned painfully by my sides.

He pushes me against the table, tells me to undress. I back away from him, try to make it to the door but he grabs me.

Do it, he says. And I do as I am ordered. I remove my sweater and trousers, undo the clasp on my bra, and step out of my underwear. He gestures me towards a kitchen chair as he pulls a length of yellow rope from his pocket. With my arms behind the chair he winds it around my wrists. Another shorter length for my ankles. The touch on my skin is shocking. Bound to the chair, I see him, see the tattoo on his forearm that looks like a drawing from a comic book, pastel green and pink swirls of flowers and birds. He is wearing a ski mask, but still I know.

And then he is gone. The door bangs and flies open again behind him.

The back of the chair digs into the naked outcrops of my

shoulder blades, the seat into my thighs. I am keenly aware of the frailty of my nakedness. I try to fasten on to other images. The nakedness of people's feet when they finally take off their winter boots to try on flimsy summer sandals. Young girls slipping pale narrow feet into their first pair of high heels. The looks of triumph, the satisfaction and wonder. And I know that beneath the mask there would have been that same look, of triumph, of satisfaction. And wonder. I know this for what it is. And I know that it is not about me but about Luke. And how he had lost. And how he would never know that he had lost.

The door swings on its hinges. A patter of drops shake free from the trees onto the windows. How many hours? There is no clock. I cannot see my watch. The electric light is exposing and stark. My clothes stripped away, my Humanity jeans and soft yellow sweater. The heavy-soled black winter boots. Beyond the door there is only blackness, silence grinding and grinding on itself. The dark forest and, beyond, the sea, seething and shushing and black too. My body shrunken in the cold. Smaller and smaller. A colder wind and then the call of a coyote and another. Calling and calling. Are they coming for me? Their slinking gait, the scratch of claws at the door, on the floor.

If I could call Luke, what would he say? I love you. I'm sorry. No. He would call the police, that's what he would do and the police would come and find me naked and I couldn't bear to think of that and, anyway, my hands are tied.

First my thumbs, then a hand, the burn of the rope on my numbed skin. Fiercely I unknot the gag and not bothering with my underwear, I pull trousers and sweater savagely onto my body. And then those hideous winter boots. I take the guard away from the fire, throw on reams of newspaper, a load of kindling and turpentine soaked rags. The fire roars to life, the flames catching the wicker wood basket. As they gnaw their way across the polypropylene rug, I close the door and drive myself back to town. I will be gone before he gets home.

Victor Sakalauskas

Wings of Tar

AUGUST 1955.
Little Ozzie's spittle and yellow-tooth breath insulted my face. A year older than me, with thin black hair imprisoned to the skull by globs of Vaseline. Eyes so close together he peeps through a key hole with both pupils. This is what blocked my way on the railway tracks in Sydney Mines, Cape Breton, in an area called Bogside.
"Ya touched Mary Lou's tits," he said.
"Who told you that?"
"Mary Lou."
"And she never lies, right?"
The railway tracks high above mosquito bogs and back yards of row houses on Pitt Road. I could see miners' wives hanging clothes in the hot dusty air, while dogs on rusty chains scratched at fleas and nosed empty water bowls.
"Ya callin' my sister a liar?"
"Just when her gob is moving. Ozzie, just go home. You don't want to fight."
He glanced back at his house. Big Ozzie watching us from the yard yelling, "Fight or don't come home."
"Listen," I said. "You can tell your old man this; we were swimming and my eyes happened to be looking when her top came off and there they were. So it was like an accidental eye touch and anyway that suit is too tight."
"Now you're callin' Mary Lou fat and a liar?"
"Fat? No, let's call her big boned."
Looking over Ozzie's shoulder, I watched Bug O'Neil walking towards us, bowed under a burlap bag of coal slung across his shoulders.

LOCAL HERO

When we were younger, Bug—my pretend brother—and me were Indian scouts, soldiers parachuting behind enemy lines, or superheroes saving Gotham. That was before we changed to an uptown school where rich kids huddled in gangs of dependency, laughing and pointing at us from Bogside. With his permanent coal dust mascara, dirty fingernails and home haircut, Bug became the star clown in their circus, and I walked away.

"No one touches my sister but me," said Ozzie, stamping his feet, trying to pump courage from dust.

Bug came beside us, dropped the bag, stretched, and forced up a glob of black crud and spit it out.

Ozzie looked at him and smirked. "How's the Highball today, Bug, get any coal? Me and the old man got a ton yesterday and it didn't take us any time."

The Highball—a wasteland of grey rock taken from underground to the surface and trucked to swamps for fill.

The dirt on Bug's face hid any expression but he was calm in a cold sort of way. He spit again and kicked Ozzie in the nuts. Ozzie screamed, face turning red, landing on his knees. Bug lifted the bag to his shoulders with a grunt, adjusted it for comfort, hunched over and walked down the tracks.

Following three steps behind I said, "You didn't have to do that. I could handle him."

"I didn't do it for you. I was just waitin' for an excuse. Him and his old man stole my coal. Can't prove it but I know they did."

I looked back. Water leaking out of Ozzie's rodent eyes, head bent over clutching his crotch, praying to whatever he believes in. His old man walking to the barn, fists balled.

From the tracks I could see the Atlantic where the white-capped waves jostled with fishing boats and the blue sky met the water horizon as one. My thirteen-year-old legs were foreign to me from that summer stretch, while Bug walked slowly and deliberate on each tie like a form of penance. The torn bag of coal left droppings behind as he walked.

"You're losing some," I said.

He slung the bag down while I picked up the coal and shoved it back through the hole. He sewed the break with blasting wire picked up from the ground and twisted the ends together.

"What are you doin' here, Frankie? I thought you would be with your new friends."

"They're no friends of mine," I said. "They're stab-you-in-the-back kind of guys."

"You should fit right in."

I watched as two kids on a wooden raft in Dougal's Pond pushed off shore with long poles, a crayon-drawn Jolly Roger hanging limp on a flagpole. The raft sank and the boys were knee deep in swamp water. They laughed and sloshed ashore while their raft popped up and floated away.

"Remember when we tried that? We were going down the Amazon," I said.

"I remember when it sank and you doin' the dog paddle, barkin' like a fool."

Bug turned his sack of coal right side up and sat on it. We watched as the boys splashed around, neither of us wanting to leave.

"You still got pigeons?" I asked.

"Yeah, I got a new one—Mr. Roach."

"The Principal?"

"Yeah, 'cause he's always struttin' around." He scratched at the dirt, making circles with his boot.

"This is the last bag I have to get and then I'm goin' over to the pit to find some birds. Wanna come?"

"Yeah, cool."

I stood in ankle-deep coal dust while shafts of light shone between steel girders illuminating tiny particles of dust in the air. Above, Bug climbed the haulage tower creeping from rail to rail, as if they were monkey bars. The top of the tower held a large wheel where steel cables dangled into a hole in the ground that held the cage for transporting men from underground.

"I got one," he said.

Holding up a small egg, he smiled and put it in his pocket. He crept from nest to nest; pigeons flew into the air and back again.

"Frankie, there's somethin' wrong with one of the birds. I'll check it out."

With his feet on one rail, his hands above on another, he crept towards the pigeon. The bird walked farther away until blocked by a corner post. Bug reached out and caught it by a wing. It flapped trying to break free while Bug leaned on the corner rail for support. The whole structure moved, black dust billowed into the air and Bug disappeared. The haulage cable screamed as the wheel turned, pulling the cage up from the pit. I stumbled outside coughing and wiping at the grit in my eyes. Bug ran out laughing with dark snot oozing from his nose.

"I thought you were a goner."

We ran across the pit yard while someone shouted, "You kids get out of here before you get hurt."

Bug's house was across the road from the coal mine, the back porch inches from the harbour cliff. Torn plastic-covered windows and summer smoke drifted out of the chimney. A stripped Ford Galaxy resting on top of an ash pile served as a pigeon coop. Birds walked along the top of the car cooing, bobbing and pecking at scattered seed. An old black-and-white dog tied to the front bumper wagged its tail, jumping at Bug.

"Down, Nipper."

The dog sat as I scratched behind its ears. There were several small boxes in the coop with straw inside. Bug took the egg out of his pocket and put it in a nest.

"Free bird."

He reached into his shirt, took out a black clump of feathers.

"You got it," I said.

"Yeah. It got tar over the wings. I wonder how that happened. This is a young bird. Tar baby, that's what it is."

He picked at the hardened tar, rolled it between his fingers and flicked it away.

"I know it hurts but you need to fly, Tar Baby."

"We better get cleaned up over at the pithead," I said. "I can't go home like this."

Bug opened the door of an empty cage and put the pigeon inside with food and water.

Back at the washhouse we undressed and turned on all the showers, causing the steam to billow and lick our skin. We scrubbed at our black areas sending grey streams down the drain.

"Grade Seven this year," I said.

"I don't think I'll be goin'," he whispered.

"You're not going to school, Bug?"

"No, the old man says he needs me to pick coal."

"I wish I didn't have to go to school. You're lucky."

"Yeah," he said.

"What was that about you and Ozzie?" he asked.

"Mary Lou told her old man I touched her boobs," I said.

"You did? How did that happen?"

"It was at the beach and her top came off in the water. What a set, big balloons."

"But damn she's ugly, the spit of Ozzie," Bug said shaking his head.

"It wasn't the face I was looking at when I touched them and they say she'll do things for a quarter."

"Yeah, there is that."

I could see her florid face, dark thin hair and too many chins. Touching a girl's breast made me feel excited and scared.

"How did they feel?"

"I got a boner."

We laughed and ran through the water flicking towels. After dressing, we sat on a bench under miners' dirty clothes that hung on hooks like wilting storm clouds from a neglected world.

"Tell me about Tarzan, Frankie."

Bug had never seen a movie and he liked me telling him about Tarzan. I told him about Cheetah and Jane, how Tarzan wears a bathing suit all the time, swings through the trees and wrestles lions and alligators.

"I wish I was Tarzan," he said. "Then I wouldn't have to live here and pick coal. I hate this place." He scratched his boots through the dusty floor. "Birds, they can go anywhere, they just fly away. I'm like Tar Baby. I'm never leaving here."

I leaned back against the railing. We were quiet for a while, listening to the scurry of living things between the walls. Like the scurry of my thoughts of the uptown kids with their perfect lawns, new cars on paved driveways and oil-heated homes.

"Those kids from school," I said. "They think they're better than us because of their big houses and fancy cars."

"Yeah, well sometimes that grass is painted green, Frankie."

A naked man came in from the locker room. He dropped one of the clothes hooks and dressed for his shift.

"Tarzan is playing at the show this Saturday. Let's go."

"I can't," Bug said. "We don't have enough coal for the winter."

"I'll help you. We can pick a ton to sell. Then you'll have money to go."

"Really, you'll help me?"

"Sure, we'll get coal for winter and to sell. We'll buy popcorn and pop, everything."

"Wow, I'm going to see Tarzan." He punched the air and smiled.

That morning a soft dulcet rain fell composing grey mud. Walking onto the Highball, dark clouds hovered above while the smell of mined rock and coal made the air heavy and hard to breathe. We dropped our burlap bags on the ground and watched the Bulldozer push stone over the embankment into a bog of orange muddy water dotted with rotted tree stumps that serve as grave markers for the bags of drowned kittens. Dirty-faced men and boys, some I recognize from school, scrambled along the flattened surface and over the edge to pick coal scattered through the rock face.

We filled our buckets with coal and carried them back, my two hands wrapped around the handle as I bent sideways against the weight. Bug carried his with ease, his body hard and sinewy after months of hard work. My hands quickly became red and sore with blisters as I struggled with the work.

Later that morning we sat on our overturned buckets and watched as Ozzie, his old man and others climbed on trucks to dig out large lumps of coal, throwing them to the ground for retrieval later.

"I wanna go to the movies, Frankie, but we need more coal," said Bug, wiping his running nose on his sleeve. "The guys always get the biggest lumps when they jump the truck. The bigger the lumps the faster we fill the bags and then Tarzan."

I kept my hands out in front of me and tried not to move. Bug saw my hands and knew I was done.

"I bet I could climb the truck and get some."

"I don't know, Bug. It looks dangerous."

"I can do it."

He ran across the muddy ground splashing in puddles, yelling like Tarzan. He gripped a chain hanging off the back of the dump truck and climbed up. No one saw where the stone came from. It hit Bug in the forehead causing him to fall under the wheels.

An ambulance and someone talking, walking me away. Then, standing in a circle of black empty dust, our coal pile, bags and buckets gone.

Nipper wagged his tail when he saw me coming. He looked down the road behind me, his tail stopped, and I swelled with sadness. I opened the pigeon's cage, reached in and carried her outside, the steel blue wings clean and soft. She tilted her head and looked up into the blue, eyes wide and yearning as if the desire for flight alone could set her free.

"It's time to fly, Tar Baby."

I tossed her in the air. She circled once and flew straight to the pit yard.

Home.

Bill Conall

The Waiting Room

SITTING IN THE CHAIR BY THE WINDOW, I find myself cataloguing night sounds. The measured tick of the bedside clock, my own steady breathing, hers, less reliable. Downstairs and out of sight, the little bird in the cuckoo clock opens the wooden door, slides forward, calls three times and returns home. The door closes behind it with a soft click. Somewhere in the house there is a creak from one of the planks, settling as they have settled individually and together, winter and summer, in the thirty-some years of our life in this place. There is a muffled firecracker sound as a knot of spruce or a piece of tamarack sends off a shatter of sparks behind the glass door of the wood stove.

Outside, some way up the mountain, an owl hoo-hooes. "My owl," she always calls it, though they have never met. I have seen him twice, in a clump of maples three or four hundred metres up the trail. He is a Barred Owl, a fine specimen. I spoke to him once in the afternoon but he did not deign to answer in the light. Still, almost every evening he calls at dusk. I remember her, sitting in her chair with her knitting, or with a book. When she heard the sound of the owl slip through the still of the evening, a small smile of satisfaction would steal over her face. As if he was calling directly to her. And perhaps he was. Perhaps he was.

She sleeps now, all gods be thanked. Her head on the pillow is turned to the left, hair all mops and brooms. Her mouth is open slightly; breathing does not come easily now.

She is being consumed from the inside. We cannot see the actual monster that devours her, but the evidence of its appetite is indisputable. Her right arm and hand rest on top of the comforter. They are so thin now, just an outline of bones with slack skin over them. I remember the strength of her and the delicacy of her touch. She could effortlessly twist the tight lid off a jar of preserves or gently carry a knee-scraped, wailing four-year-old from the orchard to the house without breaking a sweat.

That strength is gone now, wasted away. Her skin is like parchment, the fingers shrunken so much that her wedding ring keeps falling off. I suggested putting it away, to keep it safe, but she forbad it. "We'll put some tape on the ring to make it fit," she said. "I have lived all of my adult life as your wife and I will not put that away."

Sometimes we talk as we wait. More frequently we sit in silence, as we have so often done; in the evenings, years ago, then on quiet mornings after the children had grown and gone. On those fine days she would get up for coffee or tea and, passing behind my chair, would trail her fingers across the top of my head or touch me gently on the shoulder. It was many years before I became aware that her fingers were always cool in the summer, warm when the trees on the hill were swathed in their bridal dresses of white, white snow.

"I want you to dance for me."

Soft as it is, her voice startles me; brings me back from old, sweet memories to this room where we wait. I go over to her, sit on the edge of the bed.

"But I don't dance!" I tell her. "No, check that; I dance like a moose. A not-very-coordinated moose."

"Please listen," she whispers. I can see her, gathering the last of her strength for this. I lean close to make it easier. The breath rattles in her chest.

"I don't mean that I want you to perform for me, dear." She speaks with great effort, long pauses between each sentence. "We both know what is outside the door. I don't want to lie here and wait for it. When I go, I want to go out dancing. But I am not able. I want you to dance in my place."

She slumps deeper into the pillows, exhausted by the effort of speech.

But I can't dance! I think to myself. Then, as I realize what it is that she wants, my next thought is How can I not dance? And in that moment, I know what I must do.

"Can you wait a minute, dear?" I ask. She doesn't speak, but nods assent. Her store of minutes is small, but I know she will wait.

I walk quickly to the bathroom and run the electric razor over my stubble. Wet my hair and brush it into order. Back in the room, I walk around our bed to the closet where I shuck off my robe and pajamas. From the dresser I take clean underwear, black dress socks from the middle drawer. The white shirt is a bit snug around my belly but still buttons up well enough. I pull my suit pants from the garment bag and slip them on, cinching them with the black belt that I wear only on special occasions.

The bright blue tie has always been her favourite and I take it from its hanger. It is likely that the gods are watching in approval, for I manage the Windsor knot perfectly on the first try. It takes a moment to find the black shoes, and another few seconds to wipe the thin film of dust from them so that they shine in the low light. I stand again, slip on the jacket, doing up only the top button, the way she prefers it.

Standing in front of the mirror, I judge that I look as good as ever I will. Take a deep breath and hold it a moment, then turn and walk to her. Her eyes watch me all the way. I kneel at the side of the bed; take her poor, thin hand in mine.

"My lady," I ask, "will you dance with me?"

She smiles. It is a perfect smile, one I will always remember. She takes what appears to be her first painless breath in a very long while. "I will, Mister Moose," she answers.

I pull back the covers and lift her in my arms. Nearly weightless, she is. Her head rests on my shoulder. She raises her left hand and places it against my chest. From a place inside me that I have never known before, I begin to sway gently, and then—so help me God—

to dance. And, not with the awkwardness of a moose. For these few moments, I have somehow been granted the mythical grace of a unicorn on a moonlit moor, my great black-shod feet touching the floor as lightly as a swallowtail butterfly moving amongst the tulips.

Softly humming "The Blue Skirt Waltz," I dance her north to look out at the mountain, over past the mirror, back around to the west, her nightgown billowing slightly with our passage. Outside the window, the water of the bay is beautifully calm, so still that the moon on the surface shines as round and bright as the other one sailing high among the stars. I have half a thought that we might hear the owl, but it is not to be. Not tonight. I feel her raise her head and look down into her eyes, eyes that shine with joy and love. She gives me a small nod. I lean over and kiss her gently on the forehead, and turn.

We move slowly to the door and open it.

The Writers

Carol Bruneau is the Halifax-based author of two story collections and four novels including *These Good Hands*, *Glass Voices*, and *Purple for Sky*, winner of the 2001 Dartmouth Book Award and the Thomas Raddall Atlantic Fiction Award. Her articles, reviews, essays, and stories have been published in a wide variety of newspapers, anthologies, and journals.

Bill Conall lives on the west side of Murray Mountain in Cape Breton. His first book, *The Rock in the Water*, was shortlisted for the 2010 Stephen Leacock Memorial Medal for Humour. His second book, *The Promised Land—a novel of Cape Breton*—won that Leacock prize in 2014. His short fiction has appeared in a number of Canadian periodicals and anthologies, including *The Men's Breakfast* and *Thirteen Ways from Sunday*.

Julie Curwin is a psychiatrist who divides her time between Sydney and Boularderie. She lives with her husband and a motley assortment of feline friends. Her short story "World Backwards" won the Commonwealth Short Story Competition, and "Jarvis"—published in *The Men's Breakfast*—won a Writers' Federation of New Brunswick short fiction competition. In 2014 Julie received the David Adams Richards Prize. "Killing Agnes Donakowski" was originally published in *Riddle Fence*.

Born in 1946, **Clive Doucet** divides his time between Grand Étang, Cape Breton, where he has built a home, and Ottawa where his children and grandchildren live. *Notes From Exile: On Being Acadian* is one of McClelland and Stewart's "essential" books in their hundred years of publishing. *Urban Meltdown: Cities, Climate Change and Politics as Usual* was shortlisted for the Shaughnessy Cohen Prize for Political Writing. *My Grandfather's Cape Breton* has become a Nova Scotia classic.

Dave Doucette is the author of the novels *Strong at the Broken Places*—winner of the Dartmouth Book Award for fiction—and *North of Smokey*. His stories have appeared in *Pottersfield Portfolio*, *Nashwaak Review*, *Hiroshima Signpost* (Japan), *Telegraph Journal*, and the anthology *The Men's Breakfast*. Dave divides his time between his native Ingonish, and the rest of the world. He is now teaching in Qatar.

An essayist on the essential aspects of rural life, literature, politics, and greenism, **Jigs Gardner** and his wife Jo Ann found an affordable place in Alba, Cape Breton, and for over thirty years they reclaimed and landscaped a backlands farm, about which they wrote in *Gardens of Use & Delight: Uniting the Practical and Beautiful in an Integrated Landscape*. "We made beautiful friendships and shall always be grateful for what we learned during our years in Cape Breton." Jigs is associate editor of *The St. Croix Review*.

Local Hero

A graduate of Queen's University and St. Lawrence College, **Larry Gibbons** is a former library clerk, photo technologist, and veterinary technologist; he's a book lover and an enthusiastic hiker. Larry was privileged to live on a Mi'kmaw First Nation reserve in Cape Breton, where he came into his own as a writer. Besides his first book *White Eyes* and other articles and stories, he has written children's stories for a young Mi'kmaw friend, some published in the reserve's newsletter. He and his wife live in rural Cape Breton.

Born and raised on Cape Breton Island, and educated at Dalhousie University, Nova Scotia College of Art and Design, and the Pictou Fisheries School, **Maureen Hull** is the author of several books for adults and for children, including her story collection *Righteous Living* and the novel *The View from a Kite*, as well as poetry. Her story "Miranda" appeared in *The Men's Breakfast*. She lives on a small island in the Northumberland Strait and goes south (Halifax) for the winter.

Hector MacNeil was born and raised in Portage, a small community ten miles west of Sydney. His career as a promoter and teacher of Gaelic language, song, and story has been heavily influenced by his experience of rural Cape Breton. The story "Local Hero" is his first published work of fiction.

Born in Cape Breton but partially raised in the suburbs of Chicago, **Carmel Mikol** is an independent writer and musician who blends the tradition-soaked narrative voice of the Maritimes with a stark, contemporary tone. A three-time East Coast Music Award nominee and recipient of the Grand Prize in the John Lennon Song Contest, she tours extensively, teaches songwriting workshops for youth, and is about to release her third studio album. This is her first published story.

Sue McKay Miller fell in love with Cape Breton on a 2001 road trip. Three years later she quit her job as a geophysicist, left her Calgary home, and settled on the North Shore to pursue her lifelong dream to "live in the woods and write." Her stories have appeared in the speculative fiction anthologies *Airborne* and *Flashpoint*.

A regular columnist for the *Cape Breton Post*, **David Muise** practices law in New Waterford. He came late to the writing game, publishing his first book at age 65. He is writing a sequel to that successful collection of short stories, *Awake at a Wake*.

Charlotte Musial was born in Cape Breton and is a lifelong "Caper." She is an alumna of St. Joseph's Hospital School of Nursing and of University College of Cape Breton. A poet and essayist, her short fiction has appeared in *The Nashwaak Review*, *Canadian Writer's Journal*, and the anthologies *Grey Area* and *Thirteen Ways from Sunday*. She is currently working on a novel.

Teresa O'Brien was born in Ireland and now lives in Glace Bay. She has sailed back to her homeland twice, on a 35-foot sloop, and later on a Nova Scotia-built schooner. Her stories have appeared in several literary magazines including *The*

The Writers

New Writer, *The Windsor Review*, and *The Nashwaak Review*, and in the anthologies *The Day the Men Went to Town* and *The Men's Breakfast*. Her first collection of short stories, *The Keys*, was published by Breton Books.

Joyce Rankin is a writer and community development worker from Judique, now living in Sydney. She has published two books of poems, *At My Mother's Door*—which became a play that toured Cape Breton—and *The Wedding Reels*, along with short stories and non-fiction articles. She is working on a third poetry collection, and more fiction.

Writer and painter **Ellison Robertson** grew up in Cape Breton and presently lives in Toronto. He is the author of the novel *In Love with Then* and two collections of short stories: *Cranberry Head* and *The Last Gael*.

Victor Sakalauskas writes: "After reading a story I wrote for a G.E.D. exam, my much smarter wife Charmaine suggested I should write. She didn't say how difficult it would be." Victor has taken writing courses from Douglas Arthur Brown, Alistair MacLeod, and Sue Goyette. He has been published in *The Nashwaak Review*, *Front and Centre*, and the anthology *The Men's Breakfast*. Formerly from Sydney Mines, he lives in the Annapolis Valley.

Ruth Morris Schneider raised her family in rural Cape Breton, and continues to be a backbone of community development in the St. Ann's Bay area. Her writing has appeared in *Prairie Fire*, *Our Canada Magazine*, and *Room*. She received the Nova Scotia Writers' Federation Budge Wilson Prize in 2012.

D.C. Troicuk's work has appeared in *Canadian Living*, *The Antigonish Review*, *Pottersfield Portfolio*, *Gaspereau Review*, *The Nashwaak Review*, and in the anthologies *The Day the Men Went to Town*, *The Men's Breakfast*, and *God's Country*. Her speculative fiction can be found in *Undercurrents*, *Airborne*, and *Grey Area*. She has published a collection of short stories called *Loose Pearls and Other Stories* and a novel, *The Value of the Land*.

Tim Vassallo is a writer, adult educator, and social entrepreneur who played his little league baseball on the shores of the Tar Ponds. Although poetry and theatre were his first loves, short fiction has become his creative passion. Tim draws upon his childhood spent in Sydney's Ashby neighbourhood, as well as his maternal family's hereditary homeland of Big Pond. His short story "Hockey Night in Cape Breton," first published in *The Men's Breakfast*, is being adapted for the stage.

God's Country
17 CAPE BRETON STORIES—CLASSIC AND RARE
selected with an introduction
by Ronald Caplan

AS CAPE BRETON ISLAND continues to earn its place at the table of Canadian literature, *God's Country* offers an essential collection of classic stories that helped build that award-winning reputation, as well as several rare and harder-to-find stories that point toward future literary achievements.

Under one rich and attractive roof: Alistair MacLeod, Joan Clark, Lynn Coady, D.R. MacDonald and many more.

218 PAGES • $18.95 • ISBN 978-1-926908-12-0

As True As I'm Sittin' Here
200 CAPE BRETON STORIES
edited by Brian Sutcliffe & Ronald Caplan

COLLECTED BY ARCHIE NEIL CHISHOLM—laughs, comebacks, ghosts, fairies, put-downs, and all-round wit—from Dan Angus Beaton, Jim St. Clair, Sid Timmons, Hector Doink MacDonald, Annie the Tailor MacPhee, and many more.

Stories that shorten the road, lighten the work, and fill the pauses between tunes, throughout Cape Breton Island.

220 PAGES • $17.95 • ISBN 1-895415-58-6

Rise Again!

THE FIRST FULL-SCALE HISTORY of Cape Breton Island in 150 years!

Readable and informative, **Book One** takes you from our geological roots to Mi'kmaw life before European discovery, and the building of Fortress Louisbourg—the island's First Economic Boom. **Book Two** tells the story from 1900 to today, with industrialization in the Coal Mines and Steel Plants, and labor's battles for a more fair share.

Book One 232 pages • $21.95 • ISBN 978-1-895415-81-0
Book Two 288 pages • $23.95 • ISBN 978-1-895415-85-8

The Men's Breakfast
19 NEW STORIES FROM CAPE BRETON ISLAND
edited by Ronald Caplan

SHARP WIT & COMPASSIONATE INSIGHT ABOUND! Short stories by D.C. Troicuk, Frank Macdonald, Bill Conall, Larry Gibbons, Teresa O'Brien, Dave Doucette, and Mary Steele. Portions from novels-in-progress by Maureen Hull, Brian Tucker, and Stewart Donovan.

In a shocking scene that turns on a breath, Joyce Rankin trumpets a woman's rise to protect her children. Phonse Jessome pulls off the tough-guy bravado of the best crime writing. Angus MacDougall serves up a comedy of good eating! Fragile magic from Russell Colman and Tim Vassallo, and remarkable brute force by Victor Sakalauskas and Paul MacDougall. Touching and comic word portraits from Nancy S. M. Waldman and Julie Curwin. A genuine keeper!

176 PAGES • $18.95 • ISBN 978-1-926908-08-3

Breton Books
Wreck Cove, Cape Breton, Nova Scotia B0C 1H0
1-800-565-5140
www.capebretonbooks.com